THE SWEETEST THING

J. A. WYNTERS

The Sweetest Thing

Editing by: Spell bound editing

Cover design: The Dust Jacket Designs

Interior Formatting: Dawn Lucous, Yours Truly Book Services

AUTHOR WARNING

Dear reader, the following book contains scenes that may be triggering for some, including but not limited to cheating, dub-con, non-con, stalking and assault.

I wipe the droplet of sweat trickling down my cheek and turn the air con up. Not that it will make a difference. The thing has been busted for three months, and the men in charge keep promising to fix it, while the city keeps cutting costs around every corner. I let out a long, heavy breath letting my body and mind decompress as my lungs empty. The night is heavy with humidity, and I still have another five hours left on my shift.

Thankfully it hasn't been a very busy night, which is both a blessing and a curse. The long nights drag out when all I do is cruise around my assigned area, watching for disturbances, speeding, illegal parking, and other traffic violations. These oftentimes are boring instances and usually result in nothing more than a few issued tickets, a barrage of belligerent insults to my person and my badge, and a shit tonne of paperwork to fill out. Other nights those situations mushroom suddenly and without warning from humdrum into a life-or-death situation.

Tonight, I have issued three tickets and given directions to a confused old lady who was too prideful to accept my offer to follow me to her home. I half wonder if I'll see her on the news tomorrow. A part of me wants to go out and search for her, make sure she made it home alright. The other part of me wants to get a coffee and get some paperwork done. I decide on the selfish route.

I'm worn out and jaded, and the lights from the 24-hours petrol station call to me like a rockstar to the spotlight. I drive in slowly; it's instinct as I scope the place out to make sure I'm not walking blindly into a robbery. The coast seems clear. I cut my engine and run a hand over my face before opening the door and stepping out into the muggy air. It hits me like a wet sponge, and I feel the instant pooling of sweat beneath my armpits. Maybe the air con was doing a better job than I thought.

The girl behind the counter is young and looks even more bored than I am, but she still greets me with a smile and gestures discreetly for me to come over.

Dammit.

I pull on my belt as I walk towards the counter.

"Evening, officer." She doesn't sound local.

"How can I help you?"

She gives me a lopsided smile, clearly entertained by our role reversal. I am not the one who's meant to be helping her out. She points to the back of the shop where five teenagers stand huddled, talking too loudly about things boys their age know nothing about.

"They've been there for fifteen minutes," the clerk says quietly. For the first time, I register the slight tension in her voice and strain behind her eyes.

"So?" I raise an eyebrow as my gaze sweeps over them. Worn-out jeans that hang below asses, fake gold chains and homemade tattoos crawling up skinny necks. This is the generation that will be the next world leaders. I shake my head thinking about Libby and Savannah, my two young daughters, and the kind of world I've brought them into. I didn't want kids, not seeing what I did at work every single day, but Libby was a surprise. I did the right thing by Annie. Later, she insisted kids need siblings, and I just wanted to make her happy or shut her up. Maybe that's the same thing.

"They're loitering." She shifts her weight around and chews on her bottom lip nervously. Her eyes fall to her hands that are entwined together.

I nod. I get it. The father in me bares his teeth and steps forward alongside the cop. I approach the youths; they look like a cartoon version of a gang, all pasted together by some dumb kid and his crayons.

"Can I help you?" I seem to be stuck on that line tonight. Five pairs of eyes rise all at once and greet me with contempt as they take a quick survey of the intruder.

"Fuck off, pork-chop," the tallest one of the lot says, and the rest chuckle and high five as if they'd won some kind of Olympic event. It's so fucking cliche I want to vomit.

I ignore his remark, just one of a thousand I've heard before. "Are you planning on buying anything?"

"That's none of your business, pig." The same kid answers; he must be their leader.

"If you're not planning on buying anything, I suggest you move on." I feel like a 'rent a security guard.'

"And we suggest you mind your own fucking business. Free country an' all, we can be anywhere we want." The other four nod and agree with a few muted 'yeahs'.

I don't have time for shit. I walk back to the girl behind the counter while the boys cheer behind me telling me to 'walk away' and how 'that's right, I know when to fuck right off'. She looks even more nervous now that I'm coming back, and the boys are still at the back of the store leering at us.

"Are there any security cameras here?" I ask, and she

3

nods showing me the feed behind the counter. Two cameras, one pointing at the clerk and till – obviously the owner has some trust issues. The other is a fisheye lens across the rest of the store.

"Can those get turned off?"

She eyes me for a second, then nods. "But only for five minutes or the owner will call and ask what's going on."

"I'll only need two."

She doesn't question me, just flicks a switch somewhere and the TV monitors turn black.

I make my way to the back of the shop. The boys all look up at me, but they don't see me as a threat, just a nuisance, and that's their mistake. Thinking that just because I wear a uniform I *always* operate within the law. Don't get me wrong, 99% of the time I do, but tonight has been long and this week has been shit, and my patience has now run out.

I don't flinch or falter or hesitate. I ball my hand into a tight fist, and it connects hard and fast with the kid's jaw who kept mouthing off to me. He stumbles back and wails, at the same time, his eyes grow large and his lanky frame wobbles in an epileptic dance as he smashes against the fridge and sinks to his ass as if his bones have all melted and all he is, is flaccid empty skin.

The other boys all look on in disbelief. One covers his gaping mouth, the others openly staring with saucer-sized eyes. One of them tries to be brave. "What the fuck, man? You're not meant to do that."

"Really? But he assaulted me, I was defending myself."

"He didn't..." His words dissolve and he shrinks away when I take a step closer. I take him in. He doesn't look much older than fifteen, and suddenly he looks very young and very unsure of himself. That's the thing with people; they have expectations, especially from law enforcement. They assume our hands are tied and they can abuse us, but when you shake up those beliefs with some unexpected actions, all their assurances fall away and they remember their place.

"I think he did."

"Well, he didn't." He whimpers, still trying to be brave. "We all saw it."

"You saw nothing, little boy." I get in his face. His brow is peppered in sweat, and he swallows hard enough for me to hear.

"The camera..."

"What camera?" I wink at him, and his eyes widen even more before he tries to step back, his back finding the chip aisle.

"Your word against mine, not that anyone would believe *you* over *me*." I shove a finger into his chest and push hard. "Go take a fucking shower and get a job. Do something with your life."

He stammers over his words but says nothing in return. On the floor, his friend is crying. The rest of them look shaken, like I've beat up their mothers and made them watch.

"Now," I step back and address the group, "collect your friend and get out of here and don't let me hear that you've been back."

They all stare at me.

"Now," I whisper, and that breaks their trance as they scramble to grab their friend and make their way out of the shop. If they were smart, they would go to the ER, but they are not. I follow them out and make sure they see me taking a note of the car's make and model. Insurance in case I need it.

When I get back inside, the video feed is back on, and the clerk has a cup of steaming coffee for me. "Thank you," she says. She's shy now, but visibly more relaxed.

I pull out my wallet.

Holding out her hand, she pushes the drink towards me. "On the house."

I know it's not. I know she'll have it docked off her salary, and I know we're not meant to accept thanks in the form of gifts or payment, but fuck it – it's not like it's a blow job. My head hurts as much as my hand, and I need to stay up and do my paperwork. I settle for a polite thank you and get back into my car.

I cruise around for a few minutes till I find a vacant parking lot to catch up on reports. I park someplace where people can see me if they need help; I'm technically still on duty. I'm two minutes into the reports and one sip into my coffee when someone approaches my vehicle.

I get out of my car as the man nears so he can't surprise me while I'm sitting down. What can I say? It's the job; if you're not always thinking tactically, you'll end up dead.

As it turns out, he was a homeless fellow just after the time. He leaves, and the only evidence of his presence is the lingering BO of a meat sack that hasn't seen a shower in months.

I'm about to get back into my car when I hear it. It's faint, but it's definitely hostile. Two voices; a male and a female. I scan the area and find a dark alley ahead. I take a few steps in its direction, and the voices grow louder.

"You ruined my life." The voice is deep, harsh and aggressive.

"You were the one that ended things, but it's not too late."

"You're fucking crazy—"

"Miss, are you okay?" I survey the scene, taking everything in. The man is about my height, his wild hair hangs over his brow and covers his eyes. His hand is wrapped around the girl's wrist and clenched tight, his knuckles bleached white. I can't see his face as it's locked onto hers, but his body language has me on edge. He's angry and threatening.

"She's fine." The man answers for her, brittle anger in his sharp voice. "It's you who should be careful."

I've seen these situations a hundred fucking times, and I feel my early finish slip away. This guy is about to put a match to my otherwise mundane nightshift and ruin my fucking day.

"Step away from her, sir." I reach for my baton, his threat echoing in my ears.

I expect resistance. I expect aggression. I expect a fight and three hours of paperwork. I don't expect the guy to let go and take a small step back. He still hasn't taken his eyes off her.

"Now move along," I prompt him, hoping this would fizzle out into nothing more than a dispute between two lovebirds that will be forgotten by both parties in the morning.

"Remember what I told you, Amy. I'm not fucking around," he hisses through gritted teeth.

"Sir," I call out my warning, and he shoots me a quick look before he pushes off and marches down the street. I notice the brown paper bag in his hand and the scuffed jeans. He doesn't turn back.

"Miss, are you okay?" I repeat my earlier question.

"Yes, thank you, officer." The woman walks out of the shadows, and I catch my first glimpse of her. She can't be older than twenty-one or twenty-two.

Her luscious red lips stretch in a sweet smile and glisten in the streetlights. Her long bottle-blonde hair tickles her naked shoulders and cascades towards a pair of tits I want to die on, pushed up by a white halter top that shows off a lacy black bra beneath. She's wearing a chequered skirt, fishnets and boots. She looks like she's just walked off some Playboy shoot, and my entire body forgets that I'm mid-thirty and comes alive like I'm watching a wet teenage fantasy.

I ignore the tightness in my pants as I meet her gaze, smoky eyeshadow around her sultry green eyes. I clear my throat. "Did he hurt you?"

She looks over her shoulder as if looking for the man, making sure she's safe. "No more than usual." She grabs her wrist and starts to rub it in her hand.

"Do you know him?"

"He's my ex-boyfriend."

My heart does a strange irrelevant flip at her words, and I swallow down a sudden surge of need – to protect her – to have her.

What the fuck was that, Rossi? You're a married man with kids, moron. Plus she's at least ten years younger. You've seen pussy before. Get it together, idiot.

"He bothers you a lot?"

She shakes her head, but the way her body stiffens tells me there is much more to her story than she's telling me.

"Would you like to put a complaint against him?"

She stiffens again. "No, it's okay."

I've seen this kind of shit too often as a cop; women getting harassed and scared in their own homes, afraid to put a stop to it. I guess I can't blame them. Our system has failed them time and time again, letting out bad guys who just go and finish the job they started.

I sigh in frustration, sadness, in helplessness. Some days this job feels like a waste of time. "Can I offer you a ride home, miss?"

"It's Amy." She gives me a lovely smile. "And no thank you. I live just up there." She points at one of the buildings, but I'm too busy looking at her lips to notice which one.

I nod, tearing my gaze away and reach for my pocket

where I pull out one of my cards. "Here, if you change your mind." I hold it out to her, and she smiles as she reaches for it. Her fingers brush lightly over mine as she takes it from my hand, and I can't help but notice how soft her skin is.

She flips it in her hand a few times before looking at it. "Detective Sergeant Joseph Rossi," she reads out, and heat flushes across my cheeks at the way she pronounces my name, emphasising each sound slowly and meticulously. Of course, I'm not a detective sergeant anymore, not tonight anyway, not for the last three months. But maybe after the hearing and probation, things will change again. I bat the thoughts away and find Amy's face. "My friends call me Joe."

"Joe." Her face beams and her lips pout in a sweet little smile. "Well, thank you for saving me, Sergeant Joe," she says and bites her lower lip, sucking it in before turning and walking towards her apartment block.

I bring my hand up to my face, wiping my mouth and drawing it down my chin as I watch her ass sway. There is something about her that goes beyond sexy. She is beyond just desirable; she is captivating in every way. Or maybe it's just that Annie hasn't opened her legs up to me in three months, and this girl just needs a little bit of water spilt on her to look like she just walked out of a porn shoot.

I adjust my rock-hard cock in my pants and watch as she disappears inside an apartment building. I'm not sure, but I think she looks back at me before she enters and the door closes behind her. I wish it was winter and the cold air would cool my body, but I feel like I am on fire, every bit of me hot and bothered.

I get back into the car, gripping the steering wheel far too tightly. I sit for an hour trying to concentrate on my paperwork, but each time I begin to write anything down, all I can see are her lips or the curve of her tits or that ass swinging below that tiny fucking skirt. By the time my shift is over, my cock hurts so bad all I want is a hot shower and quick wank before bed.

I drive home thinking about Annie and the girls, wondering if my wife would let me steal five minutes with her in the bedroom before the girls need breakfast.

I notice the car, even though I want to pretend that I don't. It weaves from lane to lane, slowing down then speeding up, braking erratically before taking off again. I let my head fall back into my seat and look up at the brightening sky. My shift ended fifteen minutes ago. "Fuck."

I pull the guy over and am greeted by the unmistakable odour of alcohol. The driver's eyes are bloodshot and watery, and his speech is slurred. Before he even attempts it, I know the guy is going to fail a breath test. I arrest the fucker.

Three hours later I am finally making my way back home – again. I park my car, cut the engine, and walk towards the front door already knowing what to expect when I step inside.

I'm greeted by utter silence. The faint odour of coffee, baked beans and breakfast eggs still lingers in the air. I push out of my boots and make my way upstairs. Our bedroom is empty, as I knew it would be, the curtains pulled open, the hot July sun pouring in. I shut the curtains and put on the ceiling fan. It starts to roll in lazy circles above me as I shed my sweaty uniform and slowly transform into myself.

I take a long shower, letting the water wash away the night and the slurring bastard who robbed me of another breakfast with my kids. I towel off, pull on my boxers and fall into bed. I dream about a tight little ass under a chequered skirt.

2

Today has been a hot steaming pile of shit and it's barely ten a.m.

Annie turned me down again this morning when I put my arm around her and tried to cop a feel, pushing my hard cock into the crack of her ass. It's always been our love language. I wake up horny, she falls on her back, I get my release, we get on with our day. But she's turned me down again just as she has for the last few months. I know she's not on her period, so it can't be that, and some nights I feel the mattress shaking and her body tense beside me as she touches herself, so I'm pretty sure she's not getting it from someone else. But she won't talk to me, not unless her face is red and the words are coming out in screams. To top it all off, I didn't have time for my wank in the shower. One of the girls needed the toilet and the downstairs one was occupied, apparently.

We fought before I left for work. She was pissed at me for getting in late again. I asked her what else she wanted me to do to pay the bills. Of course, she threw in the fact that I should have finished high school and gone to some prestigious university, maybe learn how to spell. But fuck her, she knew my circumstances. I told her that if I was doing such a shit job maybe *she* should get her own fucking job. She looked at me for a long moment before she hissed that her job was the most important – raising our girls – of course. There was no replying to that one.

My gaze roams the room and lands on the spider web attached to the bottom of Ben's seat. He hasn't noticed it in the two weeks it's been there. There's some kind of dead animal trapped inside. I stare at the cocooned corpse and wonder how long it tried to fight before it succumbed to its inevitable death. How long it tried to fly or jump away from the sticky webs that held it as it watched the rest of the world go by, until eventually, it gave in, overwhelmed by the impossibility of the task. At what point did its survival instinct buckle? When did it give up? When did it determine that enough is enough? When will I?

I drag my gaze away from the web and try to focus on the heap of papers in front of me. A thin film of sweat coats my skin, trapping wisps of hair against my forehead and sticking my shirt to my body. Sun pours through the large windows at the other end of the room making the office feel like an oven. I peel my tongue off my palate, lick my dry lips and attempt to close a few loose ends in my lethargic, barely legible handwriting.

"How's it going, Rossi?" My head jerks up to see Sergeant Williams hovering like an unwanted stray near my desk. He's only two years older than I am but looking at him you'd never know it. His overindulgence in burgers, fish and chips and bourbons have his three chins hanging over his collar, his brow perpetually oily, and his uniforms covered in sweat as he moves his overbearing gait awkwardly around the station. He lives his life as if to dispel any suggestion that "fat" should be auto linked to "jolly". He is the most sullen and cynical bastard I've ever met and never sugar-coats anything that isn't edible. I appreciate that about the guy. It's honest, and it's his best quality if you ask me.

"Shit, as you can tell."

His piggy eyes look over my desk and a 'fuck you' smile creeps over his features. "Good."

I know it's a jab about what happened. Everyone still has a stick up their ass about that. "Fuck off," I hiss through my tight jaw, and the fucker chuckles as he turns to step away, but his bulk crashes against my desk and the clumsy fuck drops his polystyrene cup of steaming tea all over my fucking desk. The brown water seeps through the paper in rivulets and soaks into everything.

I push off and away from my desk to reach for some tissue paper and my chair clanks on the floor. Every head on the floor turns towards me as I pat at the files in a flustered hurry. Williams is trying to help, but he's slow and his movements only serve to smear more of the sticky drink all over my desk.

He apologises once before leaving me to the remains of my files. I pick up a sheet and it crumbles in my hands, the frail paper dissolving with the moisture.

Fuck.

I rescue what I can and the realisation I will need to fill in even more paperwork about this incident and will have to go through each file to see what damage has been done slowly sinks in. I push my palms into my eyes and rub furiously, trying to contain the rage that's been building inside me all morning. When the phone at my desk goes off, I stare at it, not prepared to deal with whatever other bullshit this day has to offer.

Staring at it doesn't make it stop and soon, I once again feel the eyes of other officers as they bore through me. *Fuck.* I grab the phone and bring it to my ear barking my hello.

"Hello?" The voice on the other end is feminine and

young and vaguely familiar. "Is this Sergeant Detective Rossi?"

"Yes, how can I help you, miss?"

"Oh, I found you." I can hear relief bleeding into her voice. "It's Amy. From the other night."

"Yes, right, hi." My heart stutters for a micro second and my mind's eye flashes with images of her tiny fucking skirt. I'm sure by now they can't be real anymore; my mind has made that skirt exponentially shorter and her ass a thousand times more desirable. I grab a tissue and pat down my desk just for the sake of keeping my mind on doing something else. "What can I do for you?" I'm short and abrupt and still mildly irritated at everything that's happened this morning.

"Did I catch you at a bad time?"

I clear my throat. "No, it's fine." I take a long breath. "How can I help you?"

"Well, I was wondering if I could take you for a cup of coffee, to thank you for the other night."

"Thank you, Amy, but it was nothing. Just doing my job."

"I know." She states it matter of factly. "But you guys always do so much and your work really is thankless. I noticed how Derek spoke to you. I bet you get that all the time." Her empathy is sweet but misplaced.

"Thanks again, but really, I can't accept." *I want to, but it's against policy.*

"Please?" She stretches out the word adding a cute little accent to it, and it makes me think of that cat in Shrek with the big round eyes.

"Amy, I—"

"Tell you what, Sergeant Joe." She pauses for a brief moment, and I find myself falling into my chair, the soaked tissue in my hand dropping with a splat into the bin by my feet. "I'll be at Federation Coffee for the next few hours.

Maybe you'll show up, maybe you won't. I mean it's not breaking the rules if we run into each other by accident, is it?"

"The one out in Brixton?" *What the fuck am I doing?*

"Yes."

"Look, Amy, I'm grateful but—"

"—Federation Coffee. Bye, Joe." The line goes dead.

I set the handle back into the cradle and look at the shit show on my desk before I let my head fall back into my chair. The fan spins lazily above our heads, moving the smell and heat around the cramped office. I look at the clock, then back at my desk. Fuck it, the city pays me for a one-hour lunch break and I'm going to take it.

3

I try not to think about the way in which I abandoned my desk and the likelihood that all the wet sticky files will dry out and attach to one another and be destroyed. I also wish that I cared more. Maybe if my day had started differently, maybe if she hadn't called, maybe if my dick didn't hurt so much. But all these things *did* happen, and I am sitting on the tube like a pathetic teenager who just skipped school to lose his virginity at his girlfriend's house while her parents are at work.

I stand outside the coffee shop like a fucking creep, watching people walk in and out. I can pretend like I'm on the job and on alert, but I'm not. Uncertainty eats away at my edges. She's in there somewhere, and I know I shouldn't step foot inside that cafe.

I try to rationalise it to myself. She's young, she was scared, and I helped. She just wants to thank me. I know this is against policy, I know that her thanks over the phone should have been enough, I know I shouldn't be here, and I lie to myself and pretend it has nothing to do with the fact that she looks like every one of my fantasies come to life.

I pat the sweat from my forehead with a tissue I find in

my pocket and comb my fingers through my hair before stepping into the busy coffee shop. The air stands heavy, pregnant with the perspiration of patrons as the sun beams into the coffee shop. I scan the place and then I see her. She's looking up at me from her seat by the window. Her entire face lights up with a sweet smile as she waves at me. I smile back as my gaze takes a lavish tour of her tight little body squeezed into another halter top and tiny jean shorts that cover her belly button but show off her petite hourglass figure.

As I walk towards her, I am mildly aware of the crowd. It's loud and noisy and public and part of me is relieved; this is a thank you, a non-intimate affair, in a place full of witnesses. Another part of me, the man part, the carnal savage beast that resides inside my chest and wants to tear her pussy to shreds is disappointed. I can deny it all I want, but I want her, and my ego dictates that I want her to want me too. The disappointment ploughs through me like a truck. I shrug it off. I'm probably just horny. Annie is bound to open her legs again to me sometime this century.

I strangle the thoughts as I come to the table. Amy is sitting down again, and from up here it's easy to see her plump, perfect little tits pushed up by a purple lacy bra. I drag my eyes away and find hers, green, feline and amused.

"Hi." She smiles at me, and suddenly she seems shy.

"Hi." I clear my throat as tension ratchets up my spine. "Coffee?"

She shakes her head. "Can I get a raspberry and loganberry tea please?"

"Sure." I make my way to the counter to order. Of course she doesn't drink coffee; that's an adult drink and she's still a kid, I remind myself as I take our drinks to the table and set them down.

"Thanks." She beams up at me again, and I just nod as I

shift in my seat, trying to get comfortable in an uncomfortable chair. My knees brush against the round table we're sitting at, and I push back, scraping the floor and drawing attention. *Shit.*

She giggles and stares at my face. I sip my coffee, ignoring the looks from around the room.

"I didn't think you'd come."

I tip my head and set my cup down. "I probably shouldn't have. It's against policy."

"For people to thank you?"

"For potential witnesses or victims to thank us with gifts or money." Of course, that's the nutshell, but really we can't get personal with them - intimate. I swallow at the slew of words that float through my head.

"Well, lucky for you I'm neither of those things, and if I'm not wrong, you just paid for our drinks, so I think we're okay?"

A ghost of a smile touches my lips as I take her in. *Not just a pretty face then.* "I guess we are."

"Great." Her head is tilted slightly down, and she looks up at me through her fluttering eyelashes, and God it's hard to drag my eyes away from hers.

I try and pull this back to a place where we are nothing but a police officer and a young lady who's thanking him. I clear my throat and plant my hand on the table, my fingers tapping the plastic surface. "So, this ex of yours, he harasses you often?"

Her smile slips. "I guess he didn't like how things ended." She shrugs and doesn't really answer the question, but I notice her shoulders rolling inwards. For an instant she seems to shrink, and I almost reach out for her before stopping myself and shifting in that damn chair again.

"Has he ever hurt you?"

Her face drops again, and when she looks up at me, I've

erased her easy smile and replaced it with something else. Pain? Anger? Trauma? I can't tell as she whispers her answer. "More than you'll ever know."

I let that sit between us for a while as rage starts to simmer inside me. A man hurting a woman is the lowest form of cowardice. I know that first-hand. My father showed me just what a pathetic piece of useless shit he was every time he touched my mother. For years I would sit there helpless. The cops would come and take him away, and he'd come back angrier and meaner a few days later. They failed her, the system failed her. Until I wasn't small or weak anymore, until *he* was the small weak one and I decimated him. We don't talk about it. She's never forgiven me. She's also never turned me in. No one ever came looking for him anyway.

The man in me wants to rage, but I am a cop now and there's only one right way to help. I draw in a long breath. "Do you need any help?"

Her smile is back but it's tight this time. "No, it's fine."

It doesn't look fine. "If he comes back, if he hurts you—"

"—it's not like that." She looks down and bites her lower lip.

They always deny it. "But if it is, or if you're scared, or if you need any help, you use my number, okay? Any time, day or night."

Her eyes flicker at me and she nods.

"Say it," I tell her, and her green eyes glisten as I drown in them.

"Call you if I need help, day or night."

"Good." A tear rolls down her cheek, and I grab a tissue from my pocket. "Here."

She wipes her face. I feel like a right tool. "I'm sorry, I didn't mean to upset you. I just wanted to—"

She shakes her head. "—no, I'm grateful." She's smiling

through her tears and the smile is genuine. "Honestly." She leans in, and her knee brushes my leg, but she doesn't move away or flinch. We sit there for a beat, and I grab another card out of my pocket, scribbling my cell phone number. I know I shouldn't, it's another breach, but I've lived the cycle, I know how it goes. I know how it usually ends.

I hand the card over, and when she reaches for it, her fingers brush lightly over mine just as they did the other night. My head snaps up to find her green eyes on mine as a jolt of electricity moves through my bones. Her hand lingers for a second too long, and once again I can't help but notice how soft it is. Her long black nails lightly scratch the back of my fingers as she draws away.

"Thank you." She tucks the card away in her back pocket and shimmies back in her seat, finally moving her leg away from mine.

"I better head back." I stand up, not giving myself a chance to change my mind. I need to get out of here – now.

"Oh, okay," she stutters as she looks back at me. "Thanks for meeting me, and for this." She rolls a little and pats her ass where she'd pocketed my card, and I get a glimpse of it as the shorts ride higher with the shift of her body. Perfect, tight, tanned cheeks that I desperately want to bite into.

"Sure, no problem." I take a step back, my cock already pushing against my boxers.

"Bye, Detective Sergeant Joe." Her sweet smile is back, and I nod as I bolt out of the shop and into the humid street. I barge past a few people making my way across the street and around a building before I stop and suck in a few lungfuls of dank air.

What the fuck was that?

I grab onto my face for a short moment and focus on my breath before I start making my way back down to the tube station. It was nothing, it was a cop offering a citizen help in a time of need. I was doing my job, and reading way too much into the antics of a broken girl who needs my help. I'm a total asshole getting a fucking hard-on while all she needs is my help. Fuck, I need to get laid.

4

The week drags on like I'm walking in tar. Everything feels bleak and too hard to manage, and the reality is that I'm distracted. Too distracted. Distracted enough to make too many mistakes on my paperwork and fuck up two cases. I'm already on thin ice and this hasn't helped, but the truth of it is, I can't stop thinking about Amy. Thoughts of her feel like a heavy weight on my chest. It's barely a week since I've seen her and yet it feels like an eternity, like time stifles in this place, the hours and seconds stick to my skin and pierce it.

I tell myself it's concern, as I check my phone again, just in case. She looked so small and frightened - fragile. I grit my teeth and stare at the black screen on my phone catching a glimpse of myself. Fucking pathetic. Her silence is for the best. Eventually, I'll forget how soft her skin felt and how vulnerable she looked, and I'll stop fucking my hand thinking about her tight ass. I shake my head, asking myself what the hell is wrong with me. I've seen dozens of pretty girls in my life. But somehow Amy transcends being pretty. She is in her own stratosphere of stunning. But that isn't it either. There's something impeccably wild and dirty about her – provocative, something that calls to the primitive animalistic instinct inside me that wants to bend her over every surface and fuck her till she cries. Somehow, she has hijacked my subconscious and filled me with lascivious desires I have no control over. I just want to help. Thinking of her fills me with a seething rage, a base hatred for men like Derek. All I can see is my father's fists and my mother's smashed face. She triggers all my base emotions.

I stare at the pile of paperwork, the black typed letters on too-white pages until my eyes become unfocused and the writing starts to move about the surface like busy little ants. My mind gets dragged away from my thoughts when my phone rings. I grab for it and stare at the number, my heart stutters when I don't recognise it.

"Rossi."

"Hello? Joe?" I can hear the tremor in her voice as she snivels and pulls in a shuddering breath. My heart trips at the sound of it.

"Amy? Are you okay?" I look around the room feeling too many eyes on me. I step past a row of desks and into the deserted corridor.

"I'm fine." She sniffs and sucks in another shaky breath.

"What happened?"

"Derek came to see me again."

"Are you hurt?"

She doesn't answer. Her whimpers stab at me through the phone.

"Amy, are you hurt?"

"Not really," she whispers through her tears.

I need her to focus, I need her to be clearer, but I remember nights like this with my mum. All she could see was the fear. Trying to get answers was too hard, so the questions had to be short, precise.

"Is he still there?"

"No."

Relief hits me like a wild storm. "Where are you?"

"I'm home now." She snivels again and my jaw grinds. I make a mental note to ask her where she was before.

"Are you safe?"

"Yes?" Her uncertainty slithers under my skin like a cold shard of ice.

"Lock your doors and stay inside. Text me your address. I'm on my way. Do you understand me, Amy?"

"Yes." It's barely a sound.

"Say it."

"Lock my doors, stay inside, wait for you."

"Good, I'm going to hang up now and get in my car. Text me your address." I end the call, shove the phone in my pocket and make to leave when Sergeant Williams walks into the corridor, blocking my exit.

"Where are you off to in such a hurry?" His little piggy eyes narrow and he licks his oily lips. They glisten with saliva as if they were the lips of a fish or a toad. I want to get away from him.

"I just have to head out for an hour or so."

"Where?" He doesn't relent. I know what he is doing, but if I want to get out of here, I need to tell him something.

"Annie just called. Some kid hurt Libby at school."

His face changes. He's never married. In fact, I'm not sure he's ever touched a woman unless he's paid for it, but he's always been a big boy and he's always been bullied for that. I think it's why he became a cop, so he can be the one with the power. Not that it ever stops them from calling him names. It's probably why he is as bitter as he is. Being given authority changed nothing. If anything, it made it worse – it gave him power while making him totally powerless. This job is a contradiction, a pathetic one at that.

"Is she alright?"

"I don't know, I was going to slip out quickly and find out..." In my pocket my phone vibrates with a text message.

"Go, I'll cover for you."

"Thanks."

He nods and takes a step back. I brush by him and rush to the car. He can put my urgency down to my story.

5

I pull up outside her apartment building, find a parking spot and cut the engine. I'm on the steps and buzzing up a minute later.

"Hello?" her shaky voice crackles from the speaker.

"It's me." She buzzes me up, unlocking the door. I pull it and make my way inside, bypassing the lift and taking the stairs two at a time. I jog up to the third floor.

My heart ricochets in my chest from my ascent to her flat, and I suck in long deep breaths while banging on her door. It opens slowly. Peeking behind it is her tear-streaked face. Her eyes widen a little when she sees me. It's not surprise, it's relief, and she swings the door open and rushes into me, wrapping her arms around me.

Her soft sobs gut my insides as she shudders against me. For a few moments I stand there like a frozen thing, a marble statue with my arms hung in the air, uncertain, before I allow myself to pat her back and shoulders until she calms down a little.

"Shhh, you're okay, you're safe," I reassure her, but is she? I guess in this very moment in my arms, she is. "Let's get inside."

She pulls away, leaving a wet stain on my chest and takes my hand, leading me into the narrow hall that opens into a small lounge area. When we are inside, she releases my hand as if I've electrocuted her. Her eyes swing from my hands to my eyes. "Sorry." She snivels.

"It's fine."

"Your uniform..." Her gaze travels to the wet patch on my chest.

"Will dry."

She nods.

We stare at each other for a brief moment.

"What happened, Amy?"

"Oh, it was nothing." She rubs one of her wrists in her other hand and looks away before wiping her face. "I shouldn't have called. I'm sorry I worried you."

It's the typical victim behaviour; excusing their abuser, chalking it up to a misunderstanding, something trivial. But these instances are not trivial, and when they get away with the small things, they start to test the waters till they get away with bigger things, and then they get away with everything.

My jaw clenches as I grind my teeth. "Don't do that. Don't excuse his behaviour. Tell me what happened."

When she doesn't, I burn the distance between us with two steps and reach for her hand. I notice the bruise forming on her wrist. She doesn't try to snatch her arm away.

"Tell me what happened."

She looks up at me through her eyelashes, barely lifting her head. "He caught me on the way home, grabbed me, threatened me."

"What did he say?"

Her hand slinks out of mine and she rubs the wrist, her eyes dipping down. She remains silent. Victims often do.

"Amy, look at me." She doesn't. "I can't help you if you don't talk to me."

Her eyes are back on mine through those long fluttering lashes and pooled with unshed tears. I slide my hand to her chin, breaking every rule in every book and coax her head up with my finger, getting a whiff of her scent. It's wild and sharp like wildflowers. I note the long black grooves of mascara through her natural foundation. Her soft green eyes meet mine, set in swollen blotched skin. She is still beautiful even when she's fragile. I swallow the thought away.

"What did he say?" I repeat my earlier question, our eyes locked. I can see the fear in hers and hope she can see the compassion in mine. I just want to keep her safe.

"He said he is going to kill me." She blurts it out as a tear escapes and carves her cheek, landing on my finger. The liquid heat spreads down my palm and cools with her words.

I take a second to absorb her words. "I won't let him hurt you."

She nods again, and I remove my hand, wiping it against my pants and taking a step back. She looks like she's about to fall apart again, but I don't have the time to comfort her. Not now. "I need you to go to the bathroom and wash your face. I need you calm, so I can help you."

This isn't how I would usually interact with victims of violent crimes, but I have to get back and this isn't an official investigation. This isn't an official anything. I need to know if she wants to change that, but first, I need her to stop crying and start talking. She nods and wordlessly slinks out of the room. Somewhere down the hall, a door closes and a tap starts to run. I take the time to look over the small apartment.

The walls are a limoncello yellow and the light bounces

off them, making the place look oddly cheery. A double-seater couch stands in the middle of the room, stacked with fluffy cushions, and a thin shawl is thrown haphazardly across the back. A few potted plants begging for water are scattered around the room along with books and random knickknacks. There is a mantle with some pictures on it, and I step over to look. A group of people posing in front of London Bridge, an older couple in front of a country house, a few other random pictures of people, all smiling, all looking at the camera. I note that Amy isn't in any of them. She must have been the one behind the camera. Hiding in the shadows – like a victim.

My lips stretch in a thin line as I make my way to her small kitchen and set the kettle to boil. I open a few cupboards till I find her cups; a mismatched collection of different sizes and colours. I grab the closest one and open a few more cupboards till I find the tea. I chuck a camomile bag into the ugly green cup and wait.

She comes out of the bathroom a few minutes later. The layer of makeup has been washed away and all that's left is the delicate, fragile, youthful look of a beautiful, scared girl. I want to be the one to take away her fear. I tip my chin towards the cup of tea, and her mouth splits in a weak smile.

"Thank you." She curls her hands around the mug and pulls it close, inhaling the steaming fumes.

I give her a few precious moments to collect herself. She breathes, the tension in her shoulders starts to melt away.

"Has he threatened you before?"

Her gaze flits around the room like Derek might be hiding in the shadows before it lands on my face. She nods and brings the cup to her lips as if finding solace in the hot drink.

"I won't let him hurt you," I promise.

"You can't stop him. No one can." She whispers it into her mug, not looking up at me.

"Look at me, Amy." Her eyes snap up to meet mine, a swirling green canopy in a heavy storm. "I won't let him hurt you." I cement my promise to her, and she bites her lower lip, sucking on it before her eyes drop back to her mug. I'm not sure if she believes me.

"Do you have his address?"

She nods.

"Write it down for me."

"What are you going to do?" Her voice trembles.

"I'm just going to talk to him."

She sets down her cup and opens a small drawer pulling out an old bill and scribbling something on the back. Her hand shakes as she hands it to me, and I can't help but take it in mine. I study the round, red bruising that decorates her wrist like a cheap bracelet, and her eyes snap up to mine. "You're safe. He won't hurt you again." She snatches her hand away and steps back.

I linger a moment longer, taking her small body in, the way it shakes beneath his invisible hold.

"I have to go."

"Thank you."

Her weak response compels me to silence. I snatch a final appraising look at her and walk to the door, closing it behind me. A few seconds later I hear the lock click into place. *Good girl.*

I look at the address she gave me and shove the paper into my pocket before tearing back to the station.

6

I call Annie and tell her I'm going to be late. She huffs into the phone and eventually thanks me for letting her know... for a change. She hangs up with an air of irritation still stringing us together. It spills out of my phone and coats my body. She has no right to be pissed off. She knew the life she was getting into when she chose to say yes. I know it's been harder on her since the girls came along, but the job hasn't changed. Maybe we have. Or maybe we haven't and that's been the problem all along.

I tuck the phone into the centre console of the car as I drive off, the air con doing its best to try and push out the heat. It's failing miserably and all I can feel is wetness under my armpits and along my back. The sun won't set for another three hours, but it makes little difference to the humidity that clings on and seeps into everything.

I drive by Derek's neighbourhood taking note of cameras and car parks. There will be very few blind spots in this area. Not what I was hoping for but still not a surprise. Very little happens these days without everyone noticing. I'll have to come up with a better approach. I keep driving and find myself by Amy's apartment block. I park the car, leaving it running and watching the door. Knowing she is locked up in her home too scared to venture out, sends anger flowing through my veins, and I clutch the steering wheel till my knuckles turn white. A part of me wants to go knock on her door, pull her into my arms and make her feel safe, but it's the other part of me that I'm worried about. The part where all that anger turns into something more dangerous, more powerful. I get a glimpse of myself in the mirror; the tired bloodshot eyes, the messy dark hair tinged with sweat, the day-old stubble. I scoff at myself.

"You're pathetic," I say to the image in the mirror and put the car into gear.

7

I promised Amy I won't let Derek hurt her, and he's been walking around the streets for two days. All I want to do is talk to him, but the kind of conversation people like him need to have should be done in dark places – out of sight. After two days of stalking around his neighbourhood and streets trying to remain undetected, I have been unable to find any blind spots, which is why I have resorted to this.

The public telephone booth smells of piss made more sour by the stifling heat. It's one of the few coin-operated ones still remaining in the city. Mobile phones eviscerated the need for them and they have been vanishing over the years. I think the city leaves a few around for nostalgic reasons and the tourists. The handle is slimy. I stare at amateur 'artwork' carved into the plastic with a knife, slot the coins into the narrow opening and dial.

"Hello?" a gruff male voice answers on the other end.

"Hello, Derek."

"Who is this?"

"I'm a friend of Amy's."

He scoffs into the phone, "She doesn't have any friends."

"Well, I'm her friend."

"Didn't take her long, did it?"

"I'd like to talk to you."

"I have nothing to say."

"I have a few things to say to you."

"I doubt it."

"She told me what you did."

"She's a lying little bitch. You have no idea what you're involving yourself in. Walk away while you still can."

"I think you'll find you're the one who needs to walk away and stay away."

"Look, I'm warning yo—"

"Don't threaten me."

There's a short silence on the other end before he sucks in a deep breath. "It's not what you think."

"Why don't you enlighten me?" I hiss through gritted teeth, "I'll be at the Ready Money Drinking Fountain, at Regents Park, at 11 p.m. I suggest you be there too."

I hang up, wiping my hands on the back of my pants and wishing I had somewhere to wash them. I have two hours to get to the location; more than enough time.

I pull the cap further down over my face and make my way back to the tube station. Twenty minutes later I'm in another borough and making my way out of the city.

Another drop of sweat slides down the side of my face as I wait. It licks its way down my neck and buries itself in my already soaked shirt. The heat of the day has soaked into the ground, and it rises from the dark path, heating my body. I can smell myself, the musty rancid stench of anticipation pooling in my armpits. I wish I had my car. The limping air con would still have been better than this muggy, oppressive heat. The warmest summer since records began, they said. It sure bloody feels like it.

I keep watching the path. A few late-night joggers and a couple have walked by during the hour that I've been waiting. I keep second-guessing myself, wondering if the guy will come. But then again, they always come. They want to protect themselves, buy themselves out of a situation, smooth things over with anyone that might interfere. It's a power play – making me wait. It makes him feel like he's in charge, the most important piece, the one that ultimately finishes the puzzle, but he's wrong.

Just after midnight, a figure walks towards me. He keeps looking over his shoulder every few paces and stops about five metres away from me.

"You're late."

"You should be grateful I'm even here." He looks behind him again like paranoia is biting at his shoulder. "Is she here?" His eyes sweep the dark park.

"No." I take a step forward. "In fact, that's the reason I'm here."

He raises a single eyebrow and scoffs. "Clever little girl that one, sending a cop." He shakes his head as he speaks. "That's how it started for us too."

I blanch a little, wondering if he remembers me from the other night, or how he could possibly know I was a cop, but I push on. "That's right, I *am* a cop, and I'm also here to tell you that you won't be seeing Amy anymore."

"But have you told *her*?"

He's mocking me in his menacing voice. My finger taps against my expandable peacekeeper still tucked into my belt. "This isn't a joke."

"Of course it is, and you are the punch line. You have no idea what you're getting into. If you know what's good for you, you'll walk away now, while you still can."

Without thinking, I react, pulling the baton from my pocket and extending it to the full length. I lunge at him. He doesn't expect my attack and falls on his back. I mount him and hold the baton to his neck. It's the first time I smell the alcohol on his breath.

"You need to keep away and stop hitting women." I push the baton a little tighter against his throat, and he splutters a little when he tries to talk. I hold it there a moment longer to ensure he gets the message before releasing the pressure, but only a little.

"It's not what you think," he sputters at me.

I hate when guys make excuses like that or any excuses at all. I've seen so many black and blue victims, and the excuses are always the same. It's never their fault. My father never took responsibility either. It was always her fault.

"You can't do this, you're a cop. I'm going to end you. Your career is done. You're done."

Something inside me snaps. Maybe it was the sour alcohol breath that heated my face or the feigned innocence. Maybe it was his blue eyes or the way he kept threatening me. I don't do well with threats.

The baton connects with his nose, which immediately erupts in a flood of red. He howls in pain. Derek wriggles beneath me, trying to get his hands to his face, but I don't give him the chance. I need to shut him up. The baton lands a second blow, this time to the side of his head, smashing his temple and rendering him unconscious. His body goes limp below me and his howls of pain die in his throat.

I look around us, sweeping the area, searching for movement or any prying eyes, allowing myself a brief moment to be relieved as I stand up and do another quick scan. When I still see no one, I drag his body away from the path; we are way too exposed. I pull him toward a thicket of trees, leaving a trail of blood as I go. He moans a little as his feet drag along the path and one of his shoes comes off. He's heavy as dead weight.

I throw him on the grass under the canopy of a large tree and tuck him behind some bushes before I go and retrieve the shoe. I throw it at him. It hits his chest and rolls away. He barely makes a sound.

Fuck.

Sweat drips into my eyes making them sting as I look down at his chest. It rises and falls steadily as he lies and moans in broken sounds. This wasn't meant to happen. I only wanted to threaten the guy and now, this could end my career, my life.

I draw in a few long breaths, fall to my haunches, and cover my eyes, squeezing them shut as I let humid air fill my lungs, calming my thundering heart. I remind myself that I am a cop, I am a father of two beautiful girls who need their dad, and that the man lying on the ground is a piece of shit. I've been here before.

I stand up, resolve icing itself inside me. There are two things I am now sure of; I can't let this man wake up and recognise me, and I can't get caught.

I pull out my baton and clutch it till my knuckles blanch, staring at the man on the ground. His head lulls and pained groans drip from his blood-soaked lips. He won't stay down for much longer. I draw in a steeling breath, listening to my blood rushing around my head as my heart thunders and spikes before smashing the baton hard against his skull, once, twice and a final blow that renders him unconscious once again.

I stare at my handy work. His chest still rises in slow broken breaths, but I'm sure I've hit him hard enough to cause enough internal bleeding and some swelling of the brain. If he remains unfound for a few hours, I can only hope the damage I inflicted would be severe enough to wipe out his memory of his night. Rifling through his pockets, I remove his wallet, keys, and a half-drunk whiskey bottle in a paper bag, then pull the ring from his finger. The man is married – scumbag.

I shove everything into my pocket and take a final look at Derek. His limp body leaks blood from his nose and ears.

There are plenty of unsolved violent crimes in the city; no one will find him for a few hours. Just enough time for the damage to set in. I'll throw his things in the river on the way to the tube station.

I step towards the edge of the tree line and take a long look around me. When I see that the coast is clear, I move out of the shadows and back onto the path, making a beeline to the tube station, pulling my cap lower over my face.

I weave my way through the dark, empty streets, stopping briefly to dispose of Derek's items before making it to the station. My stomach churns and my jaw clenches, and I fall into an empty seat. Bile threatens to burn its way up my throat, but I swallow it down despite the rising dread inside me. I draw in long sharp breaths and close my eyes, letting my head fall back. It lulls with the shuddering train as flashes of my father and Derek mould into one inside my brain. This time didn't feel as bad as the first.

By the time I get to my stop, some of the tension in my body has leaked out. All I did tonight was take a creep off the streets, and the more I think about it, the more it occurs to me that I don't feel bad for striking him, for possibly ending his life or disabling him on a permanent basis. All I care about is me. Getting caught isn't an option.

When I get home, I strip off my clothes, discarding them on the floor, then crawl into bed and clutch Annie's body, pulling her into me as my fingers dig into her flesh. I seek her warmth, her softness, her comfort. She moans a little as she shuffles back against me, her ass pressing against my cock. Her wet hair tickles my face, freshly washed and smelling like her floral shampoo. I can't help myself. My body is full of tension and anger and I crave release.

My hand slips under her shirt then slithers up along her belly till I cup her large breast and begin to roll her nipple between my fingers. She moans as her ass grinds against my cock and for once, she doesn't stop my advances. Fully awake now, she doesn't turn to me, doesn't say a word as I keep teasing her, only her body responds to mine, the familiarity of it, the need for touch, for release. I force down her pyjama shorts and underwear, exposing her ass and sweet pussy, then push down my boxers, just enough to let my cock fall out. I'm inside my wife in seconds as I bite the back of her neck and plough into her wetness. I need relief. I don't know what she needs, but she meets me stroke for stroke.

I know I should think about her needs, I know it's been a long time since we've been together like this, but all I think about is the sound my baton made as it connected with Derek's face. The way his face exploded as I struck him again and again. The more I think about it, the more desperate I become, more consumed in my anger and need. I dig my fingers deeper into her hip, knowing my nails are clawing her skin. I pinch her nipple hard, too hard as I pound into her pussy. She moans, but I can't tell if it's in pleasure or pain, and my grip keeps tightening and my hammering strokes smash relentlessly into her. I come hard and fast, biting down my release, silencing myself as my body juts and shivers.

She doesn't say a word as I pull out of her and find peace in sleep.

8

I spend the morning surfing the news channels looking for a story about a man found in Regents Park. There's nothing mentioned. He'll be another John Doe till they identify him, or his wife goes looking for him.

I'm uneasy and edgy as I step into the station, paranoia eating away at my skin like fire ants, feeling invisible stares and hearing unspoken whispers. I am grateful when I get into my car and go on patrol, milling the day away on petty jobs, breaking up a few would-be fights and overseeing traffic violations.

It's lunchtime by the time I get a few minutes to myself. I pull out my burner phone, staring at it for a long while. I know I should stay quiet. I know saying anything could be incriminating, but she deserves to know. I *want* her to know.

My heart kicks a little harder when she picks up. "Hello?"

I attempt to remain professional. "Hi, Amy, it's officer Rossi."

"Hi, Joe."

I can't help the smile that forces its way across my face. I like that she uses my name. I clear my throat and wipe the smile from my face, trying to think instead of how it felt to be inside my wife this morning. "I just wanted to let you know that Derek isn't going to bother you anymore. You're safe."

"Did you... hurt him?" Her voice stutters a little.

"We had a conversation." That part is true.

"Thank you so much. I don't know how to thank you."

"It's part of the job." It's not. Not stalking a man for days and rendering him unconscious, leaving him for dead. But she doesn't have to know any of that.

"I wish there was some way I could thank you."

"It's not necessary, really."

"Can I take you out for a drink?"

"No, really, it's not a problem." I force my mind on the feel of my wife's wet pussy and not the way Amy touched my hand at the coffee shop and how soft her skin felt.

"Please?" She whines a little, like my girls do when they want something desperately and are trying to melt my resolve.

"Amy..."

"Please?"

I sigh. What's the harm in seeing her one last time? "Okay, my shift ends at five."

"Great." She sounds excited, and my heart flutters in my chest. She gives me a time and an address.

When I hang up, I pick up my other phone and stare at it for a minute before I call Annie.

"Hey." She sounds almost cheerful when she picks up.

"Hey." I sigh, and I know she already knows what I'm going to say.

"How late?"

"I'll be home by seven to put the girls to bed, and maybe you and I can watch a movie or something?"

"That sounds nice." I can tell she doesn't believe me. I've disappointed her too many times before.

"I'll be home by seven," I reiterate.

"Okay, be safe." She hangs up. I try to remember when the last time was we told each other we loved one another. There was a time I'd tell her every day and mean it. I still love her, it's just a little jaded, but it's there. I know it is. I'll make sure to tell her tonight.

My shift drags on as it usually does, and by the time I get to the pub, it's just after six. It gives me thirty minutes with Amy. Probably thirty minutes too long, but I said I'd go, so I will. It's just a 'thank you' drink after all.

The Kings Arms is bustling when I walk inside. Men in suits and women in business attire having their after-work drinks, couples draped on one another like they can't stand not touching each other for a minute longer, and the regulars – you can always spot them – they command the attention of the bartender, explaining to them how to do their jobs, regaling them with some story about their day, and getting pissy when their glass stands empty for too long.

I scan the pub and find Amy sitting in a booth in the back. She spots me coming over and stands up to greet me. My heart wobbles in my chest when I see her, and my cock comes to life in my pants. She is wearing a tight black camisole dress that is way too short and shows off her beautiful long legs which are covered in fishnet stockings. All she has to do is bend in any direction and I'd know the colour of her underwear. I give her a tight-lipped smile.

"You made it."

"Yeah, work ran late."

"Let me buy you a drink."

"Just a half-pint please. I can't stay long."

She nods and leaves me to sit down. She probably wouldn't even be looking at me if she knew what I did, let alone offering me a drink, but she doesn't, and as she approaches the bar and leans over it to get the attention of the barman, all I can look at is the hem of her dress rising, slipping up inch by inch.

When she spins around with our drinks in her hands, I snatch my eyes away and scan the room, noticing the looks she's getting. I'm not surprised. But a demon of jealousy scrapes a finger along the inside of my stomach, green-eyed and hungry. I silence it, telling myself I don't care, and why should I? I am a married man, a father, a police officer. This is nothing.

She puts a glass in front of me and holds up her own. It looks pink and sweet. It suits her. I hold my drink up and she brings her glass to mine. Her smile is contagious, and I return it as I take a long gulp from the cold drink, trying to find moisture in my suddenly dry mouth. She looks at me, amused, and takes a delicate sip from hers. Setting her glass down, her tongue darts out of her mouth and she licks the moisture from her red lips, and fuck me, for a brief solitary moment I want to be a 20-year-old man again, without a wife or kids, with the freedom to take her home and roll that dress up over her ass and fuck her with those fishnet stockings still on.

"I can't stay long." My voice is hoarse as I repeat the sentiment, uncertain if I am talking to her or myself.

"It's fine, I'm just happy to see you. I can't thank you enough for getting Derek off my back."

"As I've said, it's part of the job." I gulp a few more mouthfuls.

She nods. "You make me feel safe."

My stomach clenches at her words and I remain silent.

How many times can I tell her it's my job? We sit in awkward silence for a few minutes. I down the rest of my half-pint and check my watch.

"How long have you been a cop?" she asks, running a finger along the rim of her glass.

"About ten years."

"You're very good at your job, Detective Sergeant Rossi."

"I try to be." *If only she knew...* "What about you? What do you do for a living?" I realise as I ask, I know nothing about this girl and yet I was so easily twisted into 'talking' with her ex. I grind my teeth and grip my empty glass a little tighter.

She takes another small sip and looks up at me through her long lashes, showing off her smoky eyeshadow that brings out the green of her eyes. "I'm a beauty therapist."

"You enjoy that?"

"It pays the bills, I guess." She shrugs.

"So not the dream job then?"

She shakes her head. "The dream job would be never to work again."

I laugh and nod. "Yeah." I look at my watch again.

"Are you in a hurry?"

"I need to get home." I purse my lips apologetically as she pouts and her lips curl downwards.

"Okay." She downs the rest of her drink and stands up abruptly. I guess we're done.

She weaves her way through the busy pub, turning heads as she goes. I follow her out, my gaze lingering on the curve of her hips and the way her ass sways as she moves. The hot sun beats down on us as we step outside, and a sheen of moisture starts to form around my body. I keep following Amy like a lost puppy. She leads us away from the pub doors and towards the road where she stops abruptly. I'm so absorbed in the shape of her body that I walk into her. She wavers as a car comes rushing towards us. Grabbing her hand, I pull her to me. Her hand reaches out, clutching my shirt. Gripping the back of her head, I crush her to my chest as the car clears the road.

I watch as the speeding car vanishes, and that's when I realise we're still holding on to one another, desperately. I release her and take a step away. Her hand remains twisted in my shirt.

"You saved me, my hero." She smiles at me, her eyes boring into mine.

I clear my throat again totally aware of how her body makes mine feel, her softness and perfect curves. "How will you get home?"

"I'll walk. It's not far."

It is. "I'll get you a cab," I say and spot one down the road. I wave it over.

"No, it's fine, I—"

"I want you home safe." I mean it to come across as concern, but we both hear the command in my voice.

She nods and stands by me, waiting for the cab to pull over. When it does, I open the door for her.

"Thank you, Joe," she says, and before I know what she's doing, her hands wrap around my neck and her lips crash against mine. And oh fuck, they are just as sweet and soft as I imagined them to be. My mind keeps screaming at my body, but it's as if I have locked it in a soundproof booth and I can't hear a word. My hand slips down to her ass and I pull her against me, squeezing the supple flesh and wanting to grind myself into her. Her tongue slips into my mouth instantaneously and urgently and I taste the cranberry. For a few short moments, as I bury my hand in her hair and kiss her back, she overpowers my senses, but as my brain barges out of the silent room I had locked it in and screams at me, I pull away, crudely ungluing myself from her. She stands there for a moment, and I watch her chest rise and fall. Her quickened breath matches my own.

"We can't." I don't offer a reason.

"I'm sorry." Her eyes drop down from mine and she slips into the cab as if I had punched her. She's sullen and quiet, and I wish there was more I could say, that there was a way to comfort her, but there isn't. It's not my place to. My place is at home, with my family. I give the taxi driver her address and a few notes instructing him to keep the change then turn back to Amy, searching for the right words to say to her.

"Thank you for the drink."

"Thank you for saving me," she says, her voice timid and small. I take another moment to look at her before shutting the door and tapping the roof of the car. The taxi takes off, and I watch it till the backlights disappear.

I make my way back to my car, tasting her in my mouth, the lingering sweet flavour of cranberry juice and alcohol. I fall into my seat and stare at the blue sky overhead. *What the fuck was that?* I can't help but feel a twinge of guilt. Annie has stood by me through so much, but my ego, the animal that dwells inside me, is thriving. At least I could eye-fuck her and tell myself that my fixation is under control. I won't allow my attraction to reduce my careful decision-making ability or interfere with my marriage or life.

Wiping my hand across my mouth, I erase any traces of Amy on my lips and head home.

I get in five minutes after seven and see the relief and joy as it spreads across Annie's face. I smile at her as I throw my keys on the hall table and go in for a kiss. Her lips are soft, the kiss is chaste. She tastes familiar.

"You made it."

"I told you I would."

She doesn't say anything for a minute, leaving the

unspoken words hanging between us. "Go play with the girls. They miss you."

I nod and leave her to warm my dinner. I find Libby and Savannah watching a cartoon. As soon as I walk in, their heads snap in my direction and they jump from the couch, throwing themselves into my arms.

"Daddy!" I hold them close, getting a whiff of their kids' shampoo and let my body warm up under their affection. "We missed you," they say in their small voices, and my heart melts.

I spend the next hour playing with my girls before putting them to bed. Their presence always soothes me, their innocence a balm for all the shit I deal with on a daily basis. When I get back downstairs, Annie is sitting on the couch, her knees drawn up, showing off her ass. She's always had a good arse.

"How was your day?" she asks as I fall beside her.

"Long. How was yours?"

She talks for a while, used to me remaining tight-lipped about my work while she tells me every detail of her day from the moment she opened her eyes. I zone in and out of the conversation, occasionally nodding as my mind drifts to that kiss. That fucking kiss was the sweetest thing. And as I think about it, my body heats up, blood shooting to my cock that's already at half-mast.

Annie is still talking, so I let my hand trail along her bare legs. They're not as soft as Amy's, but I know my way around them. Annie doesn't stop talking, but her body softens. She drops her legs to the floor, giving me access to more of her. I keep trailing long lines up her thigh, circling the knee then moving back to her thigh. We're both watching the screen. Annie has finally stops talking.

My hand drifts to the inside of her thigh, and I slide my fingers up and down, feeling the slight movement of her

47

body as she opens herself just a little wider. When my fingers slip into her shorts and brush over her pussy, she doesn't push me away. I pull away again over her thigh and back over her pussy. My eyes jerk to hers, hooded and dark and full of invitation. I sink my fingers into her underwear and run them along her wet pussy. She moans and spreads her legs farther apart, granting me access. I pull my fingers away and roll off the couch, falling to my knees in front of my wife. Her skin is flushed and red, and her chest is already rising and falling in an uneven breath. I wish she'd put her hair down.

Gripping her pyjama shorts, I yank them off with her underwear, discarding them on the messy floor. I pull apart her thicker thighs, remembering Amy's creamy soft skin. Her petite stick-like legs and rounded ass and I groan at the prospect of her. The sound excites my wife, and she opens wider still. Clutching Annie's ass, I bring her to the edge of the couch and bury myself in her pussy, wondering what Amy might sound like, taste like. I can't get her out of my head. All I see is her slender body, and all I taste is cranberry as my wife moans while my tongue teases and my mouth sucks and my fingers sink in and out of her.

There was a time all I could think about was Annie, and parts of me still love her. She's smart and intelligent and laughs at my jokes, and she is an amazing mother to our girls. It's the attraction that's missing these days. And I don't know if it's because she's been pushing me away or because we've been together twelve years. I guess it doesn't matter now as she grinds her pussy on my face and whimpers, because all I can picture is Amy's long legs in her striped socks and long boots and those tiny tops that push her tits up. Annie grips my head and tears through my skull with her fingernails as she fucks my mouth and comes with a final subdued moan. Her legs lock around me like a constrictor.

When she finally releases me, I look up at her, her body is slightly limp and she has a dopey smile on her face as if she's been drugged. It's sexy as hell. She gives me a goofy smile and watches as I undo my belt. I can't wait to sink into her warm soaking pussy.

I pull my cock out. I'm hard as fuck and desperate to be inside her when she shoots up off the couch. "Not here, Joe." She starts walking away.

"Come on, it's fine, they're sleeping."

"They might come down and see us, just come up to bed." She's already pulled up her pants, and I know her underwear is probably soaking up all that wetness I just created. Fucking bed. Just once I want to wrap my wife's ankles over my neck as I fuck her on the edge of our couch. I sigh, my cock deflating, but only a little.

I follow Annie up the stairs and close the door behind me when I get up to our bedroom. She's lying on her back, legs wide open and ready. I guess I'll be fucking her in the missionary position – again.

9

The week goes by quickly. Annie seems happier, more pliable. She's being affectionate again, letting me into her space and her pussy. I've been coming home early and trying to be the man Annie wants me to be, needs me to be. The one I vowed I could be when I put that ring around her finger and promised her forever.

Work has been mostly uninteresting and uneventful, and despite me keeping my ear to the ground, I have discovered nothing new about Derek. No news reports about a man being mugged or beaten in Regents Park, not a whisper or a murmur of a missing man, and my name hasn't passed the inspector's lips all week.

I relax into things, ease into them, my paperwork no longer so daunting, my peers no longer a threat. The only shadow that follows me is Amy. Thoughts of her linger inside me and come up to play when I touch my wife, ugly-beautiful fantasies that have me hard and needing – *demanding*. I am consumed by them, and I allow them to burn me when I'm inside Annie till they are nothing more than echoes of my orgasm.

I pack up for the day and head out of the station. The

sun beats angrily at the back of my neck, burning it with the afternoon fury. Beads of sweat collect on my hairline as I get into my car and start the drive home. My phone goes off and I peek at the screen. Annie. She needs me to stop at the Tesco and grab a few things for her.

Sighing, I turn into the packed parking lot and drive around for five minutes till I find a spot. Irritation climbs up my spine as I slam my door and lumber into the shop; not what I want to be doing after a long shift.

The shop is full of the usual suspects; screaming kids chased by haggard parents, school kids trying to be cool, and the occasional bachelor buying single-serve meals to last a week. Some pop song plays on the generic Tesco radio station. At least the air con is blasting.

I drag my shopping basket around, going through Annie's list, the weight of the groceries starting to weigh on my forearm. I reach for a chocolate bar even though it's not on the list. Annie will be pissed. She's mentioned my love affair with chocolate and my growing waistline. Fuck it. I throw the bar into the basket and turn away when I collide with a smaller body. The girl skids a little, stumbles and grabs my arm to steady herself. When I look up, I am staring into two green pools.

"Amy?"

"Joe." Her face brightens, and she smiles at me. "You saved me, again." Her smile stretches a little more, and a shiver wracks through my body as I remember the last time I saved her. Releasing my arm, she tucks away an errant hair that escaped her messy bun during our collision. Her gathered hair shows off her long neck which is decorated by a thin black choker with a half-moon.

I take a small step back and rip my gaze away from her neck before finding her eyes again. "What are you doing here?"

"Getting food?" She says it like a question as if it is obvious, but she doesn't live near this side of the city. I eye her basket, a strange collection of items, as if she'd randomly thrown them into her basket without much thought.

"But what are you doing *here*?"

"Oh." She shrugs. "I was visiting a friend."

"A friend?" My stomach coils at the thought.

"Yes." She doesn't elaborate, but her cheeks flush and her eyes fall to the floor for a second. The knot in my stomach tightens and the demon inside me stiffens. I draw in a long breath and release it, feigning indifference.

We stand staring at one another for a lingering moment. I know I should walk away. I know that her presence distracts me and that I can't stop drinking cranberry juice since that kiss. But I don't. Instead, I find a way to spend more time with her.

"How are you getting home?"

"I was going to catch the tube." She's following me down the aisle as I keep walking, wanting this shopping trip to be done.

"How about I give you a lift? That looks heavy."

"That would be great." Her face beams at me and God, she's gorgeous when she smiles.

I skip over the tampons on the list. I'll tell Annie they didn't have her size. I lie to myself just like I am going to lie to my wife. The truth is, I just don't want this girl thinking about me with another woman. As ridiculous as it is, she's seen the ring on my finger, she knows, and despite this, I don't want to keep it at the forefront of her mind.

I finish the shop and lead us to my car. Her short skirt rides up her thigh as she slides in, and my skin suddenly feels too tight for my body.

"So, how have you been?" I make small talk, realising I'm now stuck inside my car with this girl and silence will only bring discomfort. Maybe boring talk will take my mind off her silky thighs and long fucking neck.

"Busy." She doesn't elaborate, and my plan begins to evaporate.

"And your ex?"

"Hasn't been around." She looks up at me through her long lashes, and my cock throbs. "Thanks to you."

As she speaks, her hand travels toward my side of the car and her fingers feather over my thigh. I say nothing, my hands clutching the steering wheel tighter as I look straight ahead and chalk it up to a mishap. Except that in my silence, she does it again, this time a little more brazen in her movement, her fingers surer, as they slide onto my thigh and towards my groin.

"Amy." Her name is a loaded warning that she does not heed.

She doesn't answer me. She lets her hand do the talking for her as it slides over my hard cock. My head snaps to her face when she does, and I see the slight drop of the mouth, the tiny little O that forms as she goes back in the other direction, stirring the animal inside me.

"Stop." I want to sound fiercer, more commanding. I know I should take her hand and push it away, but I don't. I keep driving, looking ahead while she undoes my button and pulls down the zip. I jolt as she sinks her hand into my pants, past the elastic of my boxers and wraps her slender fingers around my hard shaft. Skin on skin. My heart slams against my chest at the intrusion, the delight, the audacity, and my cock pulses in her hand as she lets out a soft approving murmur.

"Amy, you need to stop." They're just words in a strained voice, they mean nothing as my hands tighten around the steering wheel, my knuckles blanching. Her hand moves up and down my shaft slowly, applying the perfect amount of pressure as she pumps my swollen cock. I swallow hard, my words lodged in my throat.

"Amy..." Her name is a long, delicious sigh, a sneaky dirty dessert on a cheat day. Her hand moves a little awkwardly as she keeps pumping my cock, and all I can hear is the blood rushing inside my body.

A drop of pre cum leaks from my cock and she releases the shaft. I let out a feral groan as she uses her thumb to slide the cum over the head and tease me. I wish she had more lube, any lube, but having her hand around my cock is driving me insane. "Amy..."

Her shallow breaths fill the car, matching mine as I try to remain focused on the road. "I can't stop thinking about you, Joe." Her raspy voice slithers under my skin.

Somewhere inside me there is a voice. It's screaming, but with every move of her hand the voice grows fainter and fainter, and the pressure builds inside me, threatening to spill. I pull over to a side street and find a parking spot, the tension in my body no longer manageable, the need for release too great. All logic and reason have evaporated, and all I can think about is that single point of pleasure and the stunning fucking woman inflicting it on me.

As soon as I cut the engine, I push my seat back and my pants farther down so they hug my thighs and allow her more access before I wrap my hand around hers. It's so much smaller than mine and so delicate, I could break it. I force her fingers to tighten around my shaft and dictate the pace, crushing her fingers into mine as my back arches and my breaths fall from my mouth in harsh pants.

My body tenses as I steal a few glances out of the windows ensuring we are alone, knowing we can get caught at any minute. This one thing could end it all for me, but I am too far down the rabbit hole, and my balls tighten and my cock swells as I thrust into our hands, fucking them, pumping harder till I am overcome with pleasure. It splinters inside my body and a savage groan bleeds from my lips, filling the car. I don't release her but use her hand to milk my cock, squeezing and forcing every last drop of cum. It glazes my thighs and runs into my pubic hair, leaking slowly over my balls. I release her hand as I begin to grow limp and desperately try to find air in the too-hot car.

Fuck!

Fuck that was good and bad and amazing and terrible all at once. Something that should have never happened. My hands are back at the steering wheel gripping tight, and I cannot bring myself to look at her. I suck in a few lungfuls and try to refocus. When the world stops spinning, I turn to her. Flushed cheeks and wide eyes, and the way she looks at my receding cock, licking her lower lip makes it flinch again. Fuck. This needs to end, now.

"Amy." I clear my throat and wait for her eyes to find mine. "We can't do this. This can't happen again. I am married."

There is a long silence as her gaze sweeps my face and body. "I'm sorry. It's just that when I'm around you, I feel safe."

I nod. It's sweet. "It's inappropriate. I don't think we should see each other again."

She bites her lower lip and sucks it into her mouth before nodding. "Okay. I'm sorry, Joe."

"Don't be... I um, I should have never let it get this far." I scrub my hands over my face and feel the cooling cum roll along my balls. I need to clean up.

She looks out the window and her hand latches onto the door handle. "I'm not far from here. Thanks for the lift, Joe." Without another word, she is out of my car, slamming the door in her wake and walking away. I want to call after her, but my pants are still wrapped around my thighs, my cock hanging out. And then my phone rings.

"Hey."

"Hi, honey, what's up?" I find my voice, calm, cool, collected – like I'm not parked on a side street covered in cum.

"I just wanted to make sure you're okay. You're taking a bit longer than usual and dinner is almost ready."

"Yeah." I sigh and scramble, pulling my pants back up. "I had to turn back, I forgot your tampons."

10

I slap the ticket on the windshield and walk away from the car as its owner crosses the road towards me, hurtling abuse. I draw in a long breath, steeling myself for what's about to come. The man isn't bigger than me though he puffs out his chest and tries to be intimidating. He uses the usual lines, 'get a real fucking job', 'go solve some real crime', 'big fucking man giving me a ticket when I've only been here a minute.'

"Step into your vehicle," I warn him. It's not even a veiled threat. I am not in the mood to be fucked with. Ever since Amy's little stunt, things have gone downhill fast. I can't get her out of my fucking head. She has consumed every thought, every minute of every day, and I feel like an addict strung out and desperate for another hit, knowing I can't have one, knowing how dangerous it is.

When I got home that night, I put the girls to sleep, kissing their heads, smelling their sweet shampoo, and remembering all I have to lose if I let things go again. Then I fucked my wife like she was an animal. I gave her no time, no love, no affection. I fucked her hard and quick and left her in our bed while I went to shower, while I thought about another woman, while I craved someone else. Annie hasn't let me near her since. I tried to apologise, told her I had a stressful day. She pretended to accept it, but I've noticed how she's flinched away anytime I try to come near her. She knows my family history. Sometimes I wonder how afraid of me she really is.

With Annie keeping her legs tightly shut and Amy out of the picture, frustration has been growing inside me like a poisonous seed, hooking its roots deep and branching out into every part of my body, till all I do is snap and fuck up at work. Agitation follows me around like a hungry stray; savage and desperate to be fed.

"Fuck you, pig," the man retorts, puffing his chest like a peacock.

I grind my jaw and give him a final chance. "Get in your vehicle, sir."

"Get fucked, cunt."

On any other day, I would have let his words roll off me and walked back to my car, leaving him with his ticket and his annoyance, but not today, not with my whole body coiled and tight, ready to strike. Without thinking, I burn the space between us, grab the man by his arm, spin him around and slam his torso onto the hood of his car while keeping his hand in an armbar. Grabbing a cable tie from my belt, I restrain him. I push him down hard and pull on the tie making it dig into his skin. Of course, he tries to fight me. I was counting on it as I kick his feet apart and apply excessive force to his lower back and arms. The violence gives me a slim reprieve from my pent-up desires.

"What the fuck are you doing?" He keeps fighting me as I drag him towards my car.

"You're under arrest." I know it means more paperwork, but fuck it, smashing his body into that hood was worth it.

"What for?"

"Swearing at a police officer, abusive behaviour, resisting arrest." I rattle off a few other minor charges.

"You're fucking kidding me, right?"

"No." I open the door to my car. Hot air gushes out, and I make sure to smack his head into the door frame as I help him inside.

"What the fuck?" He is still swearing as I slam the door behind him and leave him to cook for a few minutes, taking my time before getting into the car. He's panting when I slide into my seat, struggling in the warm air, his hairline soaked with sweat and his red shirt now a dark maroon covered in rivulets of moisture.

"What the fuck, man? I am going to report you for this."

I ignore him as I start the engine and let my head fall back onto the headrest for a brief second as for the hundredth time today, I think about that sweet moment when Amy's lithe fingers curled around my shaft, how her perfume filled my nostrils and how I fucked her hand. I let out an involuntary groan as my cock hardens and the man in the back sneers.

"I'd also groan if I was a pig like you. Oink oink."

I drown him out with thoughts of Amy while driving him back to the station.

11

People seem to be walking on eggshells around me, seemingly aware that I'm about to snap but unsure why. Not Sergeant Williams, though. He doesn't give two shits about my feelings or anyone else's, and any talkback he deflects like it bounces off him and vanishes into the universe.

He hovers over my desk, crumbs raining down onto my files as he bites into another dry biscuit, crunching loudly. I close my eyes and breathe deeply, fighting the urge to pick up a pen and stab him in the neck. When he says nothing for a few minutes, my head shoots up and I stare at him. His uniform is covered in a trail of white crumbs, and a red stain marks the corner of his mouth. I can't hide my grimace. "What?" I finally snap at him.

His mouth curls in a slow smile and he shoves another biscuit into his mouth, struggling to swallow the dry crumbs that coat his tongue. "We've got Izzy."

I stare at him for a long moment, taking in his words. "Izzy?"

"Yup."

"When?" I jump out of my seat.

"They're bringing him in now."

Isadore 'Izzy' Galanis is a piece of human trash, one we have been trying to put away for years. He's also the reason I am no longer a detective sergeant. The problem with Izzy is that he knows how to throw his minions under the bus and keep his own hands clean. We know the guy is responsible for multiple executions of other gang members, the distribution of drugs on the streets, illegal weapons trade and assault, mainly on women who tend to be too scared and too broken by him by the time we get our hands on them. Calling him trash is an insult to trash. The difference between knowing and proving is a thick red line of paperwork and legalities.

"What did they get him on?" I round my desk and, like a group of other officers, make my way to the hallway.

"Everything." I turn and look quizzically at Williams. "His number two turned and gave us *everything*. Turns out blood isn't thicker than ass." He bursts out into a sardonic laugh, and I raise an eyebrow still wanting more. "Izzy fucked his girl. Turns out he wasn't into sharing."

I have a million questions. Even though I'm no longer on the case, I worked it for three years, putting endless hours and time into it. I was just as invested as every other guy in the team, and their victory is partly mine.

I think back to the day I broke everything. Parts of me still swell with foolish, immature pride. Breaking Izzy's nose felt worth it. Still does every now and then. Despite my punishment, despite the demotion, for a brief moment in time, that man cowered at my feet with blood dripping down his chin and onto my shoes, his eyes glistening with tears and his loyal posse of pussies watching me beat him down. He shouldn't have said what he said about my family, and I should have known better, but it scared me, and I had to strike. It's a survival mechanism imprinted on my DNA.

He didn't press charges; he didn't need to. He knew he'd won and I'd be out of his way for good. He goaded me and, like an idiot, I fell for it.

A hollow angry breath leaves me as the doors to the station burst open and there he is, an arrogant smirk on his bearded face, his tattooed arms cuffed behind his back. Some of the guys clap and cheer as he's marched across the hall and towards the interview rooms in the back. Our eyes lock, if only for a second, and he sneers. Obviously, he remembers me. How could he forget? I left a permanent reminder on his face so that whenever he looks in the mirror, he'd remember that day.

Inspector Young appears from his office and tells us to break it up, sending us back to our desks, like schoolboys in detention. I linger a moment longer, watching Izzy get dragged down the hall before the door slams behind him.

The first thing I notice each time I walk back into our offices is the faint smell of cigarette smoke and sweat. There is some kind of artificial chemical the cleaners use at night to try and hide it but it's still there, soaked into the walls. I walk towards my desk, passing by my fellow officers; they're whispering excitedly about the arrest. Every single man and woman in this room understands what a big deal this is. A prickle of irritation slithers under my skin, knowing a few of them will get a well-earned promotion, but I won't be one of them. Izzy should have been my meal ticket, instead, he was my fall from grace.

Falling back into my chair, I stare at the fan overhead making lazy circles above me and pushing the hot pungent air around, when Williams re-appears. For such a large man, he treads quietly. I don't look at him.

"We'll be going to The Dog after work."

I groan and scrub a hand over my face. "Not that piece-of-shit place. It's going to be full of drunk kids."

"And you'll be off duty and having a drink. Seems like you could use one... or ten." I eye him, and he stares back, unfazed. He's not wrong. I *could* use a few drinks, but I hate The Dog – dingy and dark with loud music upstairs and kids ten years my junior reminding me of all the things I haven't done in years. "Come have a celebratory drink. You've earned it."

I nod and reach for my phone. "I'll call Annie."

"Do that." He winks and leaves me to my devices.

Once he's gone, I dial.

"Hi." Her voice is muted, almost fearful. She's been timid around me again. I grit my teeth, wanting desperately not to be the man she's afraid I'll become.

"Hey, we got Izzy." I don't give her details; I never have. She can't know much, but she knows the name and understands the impact of this arrest.

"Congratulations."

"Thanks." We're silent for a brief moment, and I wonder how it is that a week ago she was soft and pliable and reachable, and this week I have managed to push her so far away that even talking to me is a chore for her. "The boys are going out to celebrate..."

"You should go. It will do you good to get out a bit." She sounds almost relieved.

"Sure?"

"Of course. Try not to make too much noise when you come in."

She ends the call.

I follow Williams inside the industrial-looking space with peeling walls and its uniquely grotesque, overbearing green ceiling. The space is already full, and we push by young, half-drunk bodies to get to the booth the rest of the team has acquired.

I leave Williams behind and make my way to the bar to order us a few pints. Around me are hundreds of conversations told in loud voices, all competing with background music that soon will get louder when the DJ begins his set. I can only hope most punters will snake their way to the upstairs rooms for the night.

We toss back drinks and shots, and for the first time in a while I'm laughing, smiling, listening to their crude jokes and following their leery gazes as they eye girls younger than us, barely dressed and baring all. It's a good night. The alcohol makes my head buzz and the conversation keeps my mind off things, dark things, things that should stay buried and lost. For the first time in days, I feel like I can breathe.

Until a streak of pink catches my eye.

There are hundreds of people here, bodies brushing one another as they pass in the cramped space. Ultra-bright tops and too much makeup, which is why her pink stood out; too bright, too unnatural in all that colour and movement. But I saw it and found her.

Her long hair braided in two pigtails secured by neon pink ribbons, her too-short crudely cut black crop top that shows off her cleavage and tight slim belly, a tiny fucking black skirt and hot pink fishnets tucked into her knee-high boots. My gaze follows her to the bar where she bends over slightly as she shouts her order over the music, showing just a hint of her plump, perfect fucking ass. I tear my gaze away and gulp the rest of my drink down, my cock pushing hard against my jeans, wanting to be between those perfectly round cheeks.

I stand up and push my way to the bar, the crowd separates for me like a bewitched ocean. I come to stand directly behind her, her body so close I can see the hint of a freckle on her back as her shirt rides up with her movements.

She turns with her drinks and her face lights up as she sees me. "Joe," she shouts over the music.

"Hi." I return her smile, but my gaze can't hold her eyes. I'm too busy taking the rest of her in. From close up, I take in so many more details, details I want to burn into my retinas, details that will live inside my memories when I fuck my hand or my wife, if she lets me near her again. Even the brief thought of Annie does nothing to cool my burning insides.

"What are you doing here?" she asks and takes a sip of her cranberry vodka.

"We closed a case. We're celebrating."

"Congrats." She tips her glass towards me. "It was nice to see you again, Joe," she says and slides away, making her way to a group of people her age.

She sets the drinks on a table littered with half-drunk drinks, then pushes her way to the middle of the dance floor already swarming with bodies in motion, twisting, turning, fused together like a multi-headed beast. She stops in front of a boy. He's shorter than me and his unbuttoned white shirt shows off some of his chest. He's in that stage between still being young and athletic and filling out into his masculine self. But I don't care about the way he looks. It's the way he looks at *her* that has my nerves standing on edge and my fists clenching by my side. He's looking at her like she is already his, like he intends to feast on her. I know I should walk away. They are right for each other; young, attractive, single, but I can't take my eyes off her.

She smiles up at him, and he winks at her as she wraps her arms around him, forcing their bodies to move as one, entangled limbs and fluid motion. Bodies crash against them, pushing them against one another, their sweat-clad bodies slippery, her hand around his neck, his latching on to her ass grinding his cock into her as they roll their hips and dance. My nails dig into my palm and my head throbs with the beating of the music.

He drops his forehead to hers, his mouth inches from hers. Inches from those soft, full lips that taste of cranberry and sin. He looks into her eyes, and I know what he sees there. My teeth clench and I fear I will grind them to dust. The secrets in her green eyes should belong only to me. A corner of his mouth lifts in a half-grin, and that's when it happens. Her eyes find mine as his lips brush hers. She holds my gaze for a second before she pulls her mouth away and turns, giving him her back. Her ass slides up and down his cock as she dances against him, and his hands dig into her hips, pulling her in, dipping his mouth onto her sweaty neck, peppering her with kisses as her eyes stay with me.

The more he touches her, the angrier I become. I want to break every finger on his hand. I want to be the one that feels her wet skin glide over mine. I want her in all the ways I shouldn't, in all the ways I can't have her. I hold my breath behind pursed lips to steel myself, let out a frustrated growl and down my beer, all the while watching her watching me while she plays with that idiot.

Two songs later and she turns back to him, whispers in his ear and unglues herself from him. He nods and releases her before his friends close in on him with knowing grins. But I don't spend any time looking at him. I track her movements and prowl around the darker edges of the pub, following. She goes up the stairs and disappears into the bathrooms.

I wait.

Amy walks out, pulling on her short skirt and biting her lower lip, lost in some thought, probably about the idiot downstairs. I sweep the dark narrow corridor once more before I move, launching myself at her. I grab her shoulder, spin her and push her against the wall, pinning her body with mine. A surprised yelp bleeds from her lips and her eyes grow wide for a second, till she recognises me.

"Joe?"

"What the fuck do you think you're doing?"

"What do you mean?" She plays all coy, her head dropping slightly, her eyes finding mine through thick lashes as her chest finds its normal rhythm again. "I was dancing."

"You know exactly what I'm talking about," I growl through my iron-clad jaw as I grind myself into her and let her feel my hard cock. She gasps as I push it right between her legs. And I let out a long slow hiss, feeling her body against mine.

Her head falls away and to the side, her cheek kissing the cold wall. "You said we couldn't be together."

I suck in a sharp breath. "Well, you can't be with that guy either," I snarl into her ear.

"Why not?"

"Cause you can do better."

She licks her lips and turns to face me, her eyes burning into mine. "Can I?"

"We both know you can." I'm so close to her now that I'm enveloped in her wild sharp scent, and I fight the need to sink my teeth into her neck.

Her eyes flash as I speak. "I want to do better, Joe."

"Good, you should, go dump your boyfriend." I pant into her ear.

"He's not my boyfriend." Her eyes lock onto mine.

"Then who is he?"

"A distraction."

"For who?"

"I need something to get my mind off you, Joe. I want you. I want you to want me too, to notice me."

My grip tightens around her waist, my fingers digging into her soft flesh. "Everyone in that fucking bar noticed you, Amy. You're fucking amazing."

"I don't care about anyone else, Joe—" Her words cut away when a group of girls come hurtling down the corridor, giggling and falling over one another. I release her and step away, already missing her warmth. I keep my head down as they pass. When they are gone, Amy takes my hand. It's a delicate touch. She tugs at me, urging me closer to her once more, pushes onto her tiptoes till her lips brush my ear. "The only one I care about is you."

Amy pulls away slightly, so that her face is inches from mine, her sweet cranberry breath warming my lips, her eyes boring into mine. I am distinctly aware of her hands as they weave themselves into my hair, tugging lightly at the strands, and the way her body feels so soft against my hardness.

As if by its own volition, my hand rises to her face, my thumb traces her delicate lips, smearing her lipstick. She gasps, her eyes latched onto mine, and I can't help but slip two fingers into her mouth she gags, her eyes water and I pull out, but not all the way. I push my fingers in again and this time she is ready. The air leaves my lungs as she sucks them in, inch by inch as I drive them into her throat, her hungry eyes never leaving mine. I withdraw my fingers and they leave her warm mouth with a barely audible pop.

My body burns, consumed by reckless lust. There are no more doubts, no more logic, no more hesitation. My lips crash into hers, urgent and needy, fire and wilderness, lust and want all mixed into one. Desire spills from us in a tangled frenzy of tongues as I drown in her skin, her smell, her touch.

The gaggle of girls bursts from the toilets, forcing me to break away from Amy and look down once more. I note the swells of her breasts and the heaving of her chest, the pointed hard nipples that tease the fabric of her shirt.

"We're leaving," I growl in her ear when they pass. My entire body aches with need, and I want to rip her clothes off and fuck her till she cries out my name.

"Okay." She agrees so easily, and I want to burst.

"Meet me outside in five minutes. Go to Vinning Street, wait for me there. There is a blind corner where there are no cameras. If you look up you will find it. Go now, five minutes!"

She nods and detaches herself from me. I watch her vanish around the corner.

The male toilets are saturated with the smell of vomit covered up by hospital-grade cleaning chemicals. I make my way to the sink and splash some water on my flushed cheeks. The cold water drips down my face but does nothing to douse the fire consuming my insides. I latch onto the sink, gripping the cold porcelain and stare at my reflection in the shattered mirror, watching a hundred eyes gaze back at me. A small righteous part of me keeps trying to tell me that it's not too late for me to walk away, it's not too late to change my mind, but I already know that there is no way back. I have passed the point of no return and I'm too eager, too greedy, too curious to turn away now. I take a few more beats to breathe and calm myself then make my way back to the table. If anyone noticed my absence, they say nothing. Most of their eyes are glazed over with too much alcohol or fixed on the bodies of women.

I find Williams. "I'm heading out."

"Already?"

"Annie." I shrug as I lie, and he shakes his head with a 'poor you' expression. "What can I do…"

"It's all good. I'll try and enjoy the rest of the night for you." He winks at me, and we both know that he'll be leaving alone and fucking his hand tonight. "Congratulations, Rossi." He extends his hand and I take it.

"You too." I congratulate the rest of the team as I apologise for my early departure and cleave my way through the packed bar and to my car.

I can't seem to move fast enough. Everything I do seems lethargic and slow. I just want to get to her. I put the car in drive and pull out of the parking lot slowly. Everything I do must be subtle, meticulous, drawing no attention.

When I get to the corner, she's there, looking fucking stunning, and her face splits in a smile as I pull up to her. She opens the door and slips into my car. I wish I could take her right there. "I need you to get down as low as you can and stay that way till I tell you you can move."

Her eyebrows lift just a few inches, and she licks her lower lip before curling herself low on the seat.

"Good girl," I say without thinking and take off.

I keep the window open, letting the hot air brush my face in the hopes that it will cool me down or whisper some sense into me. It does neither, and I find it hard to keep to the speed limit. To stop at every red light, to wait, to keep waiting till I can touch her. I still haven't done anything wrong. I can still stop and let her out and send her home and go home to Annie, to our bed, to my life, but all I taste is cranberry on my lips and it tastes like more.

I pull into the industrial area. It's deserted and derelict, and although there's a chance of a tweaker coming to the window to see what he can steal, the cameras in this area have been broken for months and the darkness is all-consuming.

I pull the car into a parking spot and push my chair back. "Come here." Grabbing her wrist, I yank her over to my seat, and her small body straddles me. Her lips find mine and she grinds against me, making my hard cock swell even more. I want to rip into her, be inside her, fuck her violently and brutally, which is exactly why I don't. This will be the only time I touch her, so I need to savour her, take every moment in slow calculated movements so that I can commit every inch of her to memory. I'm not going to be some guy she fucked in a car, a pathetic one-night stand that's barely a memory. I'm going to imprint myself on her skin so that she remembers that she can always do better.

Her sweet lips suck on mine, and she gathers my lower lip between her teeth, tugging gently. I pull away from her mouth and gather her braids in my fist, pulling her head to one side and exposing her long neck. I pepper kisses on her skin, tasting her sweat and the aftershave the fuckwit that danced with her left all over her. I'm about to erase any trace of him. Permanently.

I unlatch my mouth from her neck while keeping a grip on her hair, then pull down, forcing her back to arch ever so slightly and her crop top to rise, exposing a shade of her breasts. Placing the crests a hairsbreadth from my mouth, her hard fucking nipples a tongue flick away, I let my hand slide up her taut belly and under her shirt, finding her bare breast. I groan at the feel of it, a perfect fit in my palm. I let my thumb flick over her hard nipple and her moan sends shivers into my spine as she arches towards me. I play some more, curiosity burning my insides, but I love how she keeps pushing against me in desperation, how she purrs under my touch, how she sucks her lip into her mouth and lets her head fall back. God, she is sexy.

I don't release her hair. Instead, I tighten my grip and tug harder. Her back bows, and I peel her top slowly upwards, revealing her perky tits and her pebbled nipples. We moan in unison as I suck one into my mouth. Fuck this girl is delicious. I want to savour her. I want to be inside her. I suck on her nipples one after the other, dragging them between my teeth, waiting for her soft gasps and delicate moans. They shoot electricity right to my cock.

When I finally relent and release her hair, she's on me, her mouth needing mine in a desperate urgent kiss and her hips grind against mine once more, needy, wanting, hungry.

I pull at her skirt, bunching it over her hips and groan at the sight of her hot pink lacy g-string holding the fishnets in place. "Jesus," I swear, and she giggles, and I can't help but push the underwear to one side and rip through the fishnets to get to her pussy. It's clean-shaven and glistening with her wetness, and every bit of me tenses as I run my thumb over her slit. She lets out a sweet little sound that has my body crazed. Her scent fills my car, feeding my rigid hardness and fuelling my desire. My breathing falters as she reaches for my jeans and undoes the button then unzips my pants. Her hand strokes my hard cock, and I grab her wrist, pushing it away. I'm not fucking any more hands.

I push up off the chair and slide my pants off just enough to let my cock free, shifting her so that I am at her entrance. My pulse hammers and my entire body ignites as ever so slowly she slides down onto my hard cock, and I can't help but watch as her tight pussy swallows it whole. I don't even recognise the noise that rips from my mouth as she sits there, impaled on my cock for a minute, adjusting to the size.

Time.

Stands.

Still.

I bottle each detail in a special drawer inside my head.

The squeeze of her pussy on my shaft mingled with her silky warmth, the way her mouth parts slightly letting the softest of moans escape. The way her hooded eyes burn into mine.

Everything on this girl is so fucking tight.

"Fuck me," I tell her through a clenched jaw, and my hands lock on her hips, showing her how.

She keeps to the rhythm I've set. Her perky tits dance in front of my eyes, teasing me, inviting me, and I suck them into my mouth, eliciting soft little moans from her and making her pussy clench tighter each time I do. I don't know if I've ever been this hard or if it's ever felt this good, and I wish I could prolong it. I want it to last forever, but I know it won't. I slide my thumb over her clit and let her grind herself into it, finding her own rhythm. The closer she comes to her own orgasm, the quicker her hips pound into mine. I'm so fucking close I know that I will explode inside her.

I pull her nipple into my mouth. Her pussy clenches around me and she moans and cries, and oh fuck, every muscle in my body tenses up. Gripping her hip, digging into it violently, carelessly. I pound into her as she pushes herself into me, forcing me deeper. I want to sink right into her, want to fill all of her. I'm crazed and frenzied as my body takes on a life of its own. My hips thrusting and pumping, the need for release like a burning fever.

I clutch her ass, trying to sink deeper, faster, harder. I pump my hips furiously, her breasts bouncing. I lick her skin, needing all of her to be all over me.

Faster.

Harder.

Stronger.

Deeper.

Deeper.

Deeper.

And then I breach the surface.

I push her down onto me as I jolt, clutching at her hips, sucking at her skin, and groaning a shuddering, ecstatic release as I come inside her so fucking hard I feel like I've been beaten over the head. Her tight little pussy clenches around me and her sweet little moans drown out my own ecstasy, and then she comes hard, sucking me even deeper, milking my shuddering cock, sending shivers of delight right through my core.

We take a few moments to collect ourselves. Her head rests against my sweaty chest as we both gasp for air in the stuffy car. I'm spent, shattered and completely in awe. I never want to leave. I don't want this feeling to end, the ecstasy to evaporate, or the warmth to diminish. But as we catch our breath, reality comes crashing down and the consequences of my wild desires begin to hook themselves beneath my skin and tug.

"Joe." She pants my name, and my stomach coils.

Her glazed eyes find mine, a satisfied grin on her face as she arches back and her fucking tits are back in my face, so perky, so beautiful, I can't help but snatch one last taste. She hums as I do, and I know that I'm fucked.

12

I wake up with my wife in my arms and a twinge of guilt pinches my chest. We still haven't made up, but I know we will. We always find a way back to each other... eventually.

Last night I snuck in, like a thief in the darkness, sneaking around corridors and stealing into the bathroom where I had to wash my cum-stained clothes and scrub every inch of my body, erasing all memory of Amy and our deeds. The cold water fell on my face and ran down my back while I sat on the shower floor and kept shaking my head, trying to make myself forget about her; her taste, her sounds, the way she made me feel. I wanted the drops to wipe my mind blank, to erase all the images of her, but they didn't. I don't know if anything will make me forget. I towelled off, smearing my guilt all over my body.

I crawled into our bed, my body feeling heavy, the suffo-cating throb of my heart burning a hole in my chest. I thought it might burn through my singlet and right through Annie, leaving her scorched and scarred. As I tossed and turned, I realised that my penance would not be easy, but that her finding out would burn her far worse and in a far more devastating way than if she remained in darkness. And so I held her and pushed away all thoughts of Amy. It was a one-time thing anyway, a moment of weakness when I allowed my lust to overwhelm me and take over, keeping me a passenger inside myself as I devoured her. But the flame is snuffed out, used and burned out.

Annie wriggles out of my arms and I stir. She stands in a too-long white shirt that goes halfway to her thighs, showing off her legs. She's always had great legs. She bends to pick up some discarded clothes and runs her fingers through the fabric as she looks at me, her face still creased with sleep.

"Did you have fun last night?"

My heart comes to a sudden and devastating halt before it starts beating again. "Yes, it was good."

"You came in late."

"I didn't mean to wake you."

"I heard the washing machine and the shower."

"I spewed, didn't want you to have to deal with that." It's the first pebble in a mountain of lies I was about to construct. "We had a lot to drink."

"Yeah. You have a lot to celebrate." She gives me a wan smile and comes to sit on the edge of the bed, her hand tracing lines over my arm. Guilt licks at my skin with her soft touch. "At least that's over now."

I nod, knowing it's not, knowing she thinks things might change again, that all will be forgiven and forgotten and that we can get back to how it was.

"There's still the trial…" I mumble.

"I think it will be okay." She smiles at me and climbs onto the bed straddling me.

I get a glimpse of the woman she used to be, the one I fell for before life got in our way, before Libby. She moves, her hips rolling gently above me. All I see is Amy. The sweet perky tits, the creamy soft skin, that smile. The more Annie moves, the harder I get, the more the images keep playing inside me like a movie reel.

Annie reaches for my cock, pulls her underwear to the side, and I slip inside her so easily. I groan at her warmth, at the memories. Annie's hand rests on my chest as her hips roll above me, her eyes locked on mine, her nipples poking through the white fabric, teasing me. My mind reels. Amy's face flashes inside my mind, her firm perky tits and tight-as-fuck pussy. I groan, pushing up into my wife. Amy's lush lips, her sweet little moans. My fingers dig into Annie's hips, urging her to move faster as I pump into her, needing to be deeper. I'm lost inside my head, on our bed inside my wife as I fuck two women at once. My body shivers as I come hard and fast, leaving her wanting, again.

Annie climbs off me without a word and closes the door to the ensuite behind her. I guess that was her celebration.

I spend the morning on patrol and the afternoon buried in a mountain of paperwork. Izzy's case has exploded, and though I've been officially demoted, my knowledge of it has prompted the supervisors to bring me in on the paper-work side of things. It's a pain in the arse but also, it's a form of closure, seeing all the filthy shit this guy has done – and will get done for – makes the last eight months almost bearable.

I step outside for a breather and a stretch. The air isn't as oppressing as it's been the last few weeks, and the blue sky is beautiful. Or maybe it's me, maybe I feel lighter, maybe I feel happier, maybe between Amy and Annie and Izzy things feel better; like everything is slowly falling into place.

I step out of the station and take the steps down towards

the road, taking a few paces out of the shadows. It's then I see her. She's standing on the opposite corner, leaning against the brick building, and her face bursts into a smile when she sees me.

She takes a few steps towards the curb as if she's about to cross and come over to me.

Fuck.

I hold my hand up, signalling for her to wait. There are cameras all over the building and around most of the streets here. What the hell is she thinking?

She waits as I cross towards her, then walk by her. "Come on," I bark at her, not stopping.

She follows me down the street and into a side street where I know the camera hasn't worked in over three months. Thank fuck for incompetent councillors and money shortages. Of course, we would catch more criminals if they would fix these things, but lately, they've been working in my favour. "What the fuck are you doing here, Amy?"

She frowns at me and takes a step back, assessing my face. "I wanted to see you."

"You can't just come to see me, Amy. I'm at work."

"I know, it's why I waited."

I draw in a long breath. "What do you want?"

"To see you again."

"We can't see each other again."

"But why? We made love."

I run a hand through my hair and stare at her. "From this moment on I'm Detective Rossi and you're Amy Madden, and we didn't make love, we had sex, just leave it at that."

"But it can't be. Life keeps bringing us together, again and again. That time in the shop and in the pub..."

I sigh. "Amy, it's time to forget about what happened between us."

"You just want me to forget about the best sex I've ever had? No way."

My ego inflates like a hot air balloon. "You're young, you don't know what the best is yet."

"I've had other lovers, but you... you're special, Joe. I can't forget. I don't want to."

"I'm a police officer and you're a—"

"A nothing. I didn't file a complaint. I didn't even mention the fact that Derek has vanished..."

I give her a long hard look and wonder what she knows. "Let it go, Amy."

"I don't want to. We're both adults, we're both free."

"You know I'm married."

"Of course." Her eyes snap to the gold ring on my finger.

"Look, Amy, I don't want to make what happened between us cheap, or offend you by saying it was a mistake based on impulse..."

"But that's exactly what you're doing."

"Fuck." I scrape my hands over my face and draw in a long breath. "Look. I didn't think I'd see you again... not after that first time or..."

"Joe! Stop! I don't care what brought us together, chance or fate. All I know is that what we had was amazing And I don't want that to stop."

"But it has to," I say with finality, leaving no room for arguments. I think about Annie and how she rode me this morning, the smile she had, the hope she carried for us... I need to keep that hope alive, cultivate it, let it grow again. "Don't come here again, we're done."

The cold metal chair leg presses against my leg as I push it forward under the fake wooden table gleaming in the light of the room. The library is surprisingly busy for a mid-day afternoon, and the room is full of murmurs and whispers. I pull the cap lower over my face and wait for the computer to register the temporary password the librarian just gave me. The screen comes to life, and I bring up the usual search, inputting the usual words.

The librarian shushes the crowd, effectively breaking her own rule of silence and forcing the room to fall into a cold stillness. Despite the conversation dying in people's throats, the room is still alive with the sound of a printer spitting out paper and the constant clacking of keyboards. I glance behind me, ensuring no one is looking over my shoulders as I scour the daily news.

There has been nothing mentioned of Derek. I have checked most days since his attack, but Amy's remark about him has uncertainty gnawing at me. I scour each newspaper, as I always do, paying more attention. And then I find it.

A small, barely there article mentioning the John Doe discovered in Regents Park. The muted request for any family members to come and identify him and the hospital in which he is staying.

Maybe that's him. Fuck.

The flowers smell sweet, and they cover up the sweat and grime that have soaked into the upholstery of my car. Annie will appreciate them.

Tea is ready when I get home; roast and vegetables, and nuggets for the girls. They jump on me when I walk in the door, then proceed to shriek and run away as I turn into a tickle monster. I grab their small bodies and tickle them till they gasp for air and beg me to stop. As I look at their red smiling faces, I can't imagine a world without them, a world where I let a mistake like Amy happen again, where I lose this. Annie chides us playfully, cutting through my thoughts, and for a short time, we are all happy and content, a normal and fully functioning family unit.

I leave Annie to put the girls to bed and step into our ensuite, stripping down to my boxers.

I stare at my reflection. Tired brown eyes stare back at me as I examine my newly developed wrinkles, the deepening furrows along my eyes and forehead, the spattering of white chest hair and the stomach that used to be flat and is slowly becoming pudgy and soft. I wonder what Amy finds attractive about this, given her young supple skin and youth. How could she say she wants me? Wants more of me? I shake my head and head into the shower, letting the heat burn my skin.

I keep my eyes open, at least for a few moments, knowing that each time I close them Amy floods my vision. The way she touched me like she had ten hands, the way I felt her everywhere all at once and still it wasn't enough, the way she kissed me and devoured me.

I want to stop thinking about her, stop wanting her, but I can't, and I don't know if it's the pleasure or the desire.

Can I keep lying to myself? Saying I was caught up in the moment? That it was just desire to have her and stop being a cop, stop being a husband or a father, just to be a man who craves to feel, to be touched by a 21-year-old woman?

But the reality is that I want more.

And there's the guilt. And it's not about what I've done, or how I had her, it's that I want to do it again and again and again.

But of course, I can't. There's too much at stake...

I find Annie in the laundry room. She's folding the clothes ready to be redistributed in cupboards.

"Thank you for my flowers, they're beautiful."

"You're beautiful." A red blush spreads across her cheeks.

"How was your day, did you speak to Superintendent Young?"

"Annie, don't."

"It's only a question."

"It's not."

"Well, did you?" She puts down a pink shirt and grabs another from the basket.

"No, of course not, it's been twenty-four hours and we've been busy."

"Surely you can find five minutes to—"

"Annie," I warn her, "these things take time..."

"How much time, Joe? It's been months! You've been punished enough. Just go into his office and demand your fucking job back."

"Really?"

"Yes, really." She puts the folded shirt down like an exclamation mark.

"You know that if I could—"

"You can, you just won't. I don't know, maybe it's easier for you to work the long hours and stay away from us. Maybe it's what you really want."

I think about this morning, how she rode me without kissing me, how her smile didn't touch her eyes at dinner, but still. "Are you fucking serious?"

"Yeah, I am. You can go in there at any time and—"

I slash the distance between us and get in her face, looming over her. My nostrils flare with every breath I take, and my heart pounds in my chest. My fists clench by my sides, and she shrinks back and cowers. "Do you have any idea what I did, Annie? How much shit I had to eat just to keep my job? And I did it for *you* and the girls," I hiss through an iron-clad jaw. "I can't just *walk* into Tom's office and demand shit. There are procedures and protocols, there are shrink appointments and psych evaluations and a whole bunch of other things you already know about, and the fact that Izzy has been put away changes nothing. So fuck off with this bullshit."

I'm panting by the time I am done, and she's shivering beneath me. I hate it when she does that; like I'm going to hurt her. She knows I never would, and yet each time I lose my temper she quivers. It riles me up even more.

My blood is hot in my veins and my body feels tight with anger that has no direction and bounces inside me in an angry mass.

I turn away from my wife, storm downstairs and slam the front door behind me.

Heavy droplets fall on my head and soak through my hair and shirt as I make my way to my car. I'm not sure when it started raining, but the day has turned dark and grey, just like my mood. Why the fuck did she pick a fight? Insinuating I was a pussy for not asking for my job back – she knows as well as I do it's not that simple. Nothing is that simple. I have hoops to jump through and boxes to tick, and apart from a few singular instances, I've been on the straight and narrow doing all the right things, kissing all the right ass to get back there – I am so close to getting back to where I was and surpassing myself, but I'm not there yet.

I start the engine and pull away sharply. Driving helps to clear my mind. I drive through dark streets, the rain pounding against my windscreen, my headlights slashing the darkness. I drive aimlessly, my mind replaying the angry words exchanged with my wife, the ugliness of the undercurrent of accusations. The more I think, the angrier I get, the more my stomach drops, and my hands grip the steering wheel, and my foot gets heavier on the accelerator. I don't know how or why, but I find myself parked outside Amy's building.

The light in her apartment is on. The yellow lights glow and spill out into the dark street as if she has captured a fragment of sunshine, and then, as if she can feel me, she comes to the window. Our eyes meet and hold there. Something passes between us, something that thunders through the world and sends a long harrowing shiver through me.

I think about going up there, about taking my anger out on her small body, about finding release in her tight pussy, in her wild smell and her soft skin. I shut my eyes, my hands tightening around the steering wheel as images of her – of us – flood my mind in an overpowering deluge. When I open my eyes again, she's vanished from her window, and somehow it makes me feel relieved but also disappointed.

I sit in a puddle of need, my aching cock hard, my body tense, my anger shifting and morphing into dangerous desire, and then there she is, standing in a tight, short nightgown at the front of her building. The rain slashes through the fabric, forcing it to stick to her slender body, showing off her curves, straining through her hair and down her face. She keeps standing there watching me watching her.

I step out of my car and lean against it, knowing that if I cross that road, if I cross that line, there are no more excuses, there are no more lies that I was overwhelmed, no more blaming it on impulse or poor judgement. There would be no one to blame, there would only be a choice and I'd be the one making it.

The rain pelts down my body and soaks into my shirt and jeans. My hair is a wet wild mess. Amy's eyes haven't left mine, they're burning with lust and lascivious thoughts that mirror my own. My throat closes as my heart pounds brutally in my chest. My stomach hardens, as does my resolve.

I shred the distance between us, giving in to my body. My brain shrivels up like wilted leaves. My hands sink into her saturated hair, grabbing a fistful, pulling and forcing her head up to mine. My heart slams in my chest as my lips crush hers. I'm hungry and angry and I need to punish her, for making me do this, for making me want her. My body moves, forcing hers back and into the building till her back finds a wall. Our lips still locked in a maddening war, our tongues clashing in a dangerous dance.

My hand slides up her body, slithering along her wet nightgown, teasing the fabric, feeling the bare, soft flesh beneath till I reach her neck. My fingers grip her throat, pinning her to the wall, tightening ever so slightly, and then a little more as I keep kissing her, keep stealing her breath away. She pushes back, baulking under the pressure, surrendering to me. I unlatch myself from her mouth and release her neck, letting her suck in air but keeping her pinned in place. Her eyes find mine, dark with black desire. I can't help the smile that curls along my face. I revel in the knowledge that her hunger matches my own.

"Move," I growl and release her. She spins away from me and dashes to the steps, taking two at a time. She could be running from me or eager to get to her apartment. Either way, I chase. She's not getting away.

Her door stands open, and she crosses the threshold. I am half a step behind her. Snatching her wrist, I spin her to me. She's out of breath and flushed, and I kick the door closed behind us. My hand finds her jaw, my fingers and thumb digging in, forcing her lips into a pout that I devour. It's like catching a spirit, wild and rare and furious.

Her hands tangle in my wet shirt and she fights the fabric, tugging and pulling till I let her strip it from my body. Her hands reach for my pants. In a moment my button and zip are undone. I grab her hair, once more controlling her head with deliberate but tempered force. It is far more than a suggestion. I pull her away from my mouth and guide her to a spot on my neck, to my chest, forcing her slowly to bend at the knees till she is kneeling before me and her hands know what to do. She pulls down my pants and boxer shorts, and her hot mouth closes around my cock. I moan seeing her there like that, with that nightgown sticking to her body and her green eyes swirling with lust, and my hard shaft sliding in and out of her mouth, already swollen from our bruising kisses.

She doesn't take me deep, doesn't allow herself to gag, so I force her movements, urging her on, feeling her throat close around me as she chokes on my cock and her eyes water. Her hands dig into my thighs. I'm already too close.

I yank her mouth away and step away from her, leaving her there on her knees, with glistening eyes and shiny lips. I make my way to her bedroom and sit on the edge of her bed, remove my shoes and tear off my wet pants. They fall at my feet in a heap.

Amy is already here. She straddles me. Her hands push me down onto the mattress, her breasts falling forward in the motion, and she lifts herself ever so slightly, making me lose my breath. I find her mouth and kiss her, letting her think for a few blissful seconds that she will get any control tonight. As she softens against me, I tense, and in one deft athletic move, I roll on top of her. She squeals as I flip her over, and I seal her mouth with a long savage kiss, swallowing her sounds. Keeping most of my weight through my elbows and forearms, I plant them on either side of her head. She's pinned down and helpless. Just how I want her.

Her eyes are wide and questioning when I finally release her mouth, relishing in how her lips are swollen and reddened. Gripping her wrists, I pin them over her head and roll off her. I miss her heat instantly, but tonight isn't just about pleasure, it's about pain. She has flayed my soul open. She's forced me into this, here into her arms where I shouldn't be. We are both sinners, and we need to suffer.

Slowly, I begin to peel her wet nightgown up and away from her slender body till it covers her face and her eyes.

She gasps. "Joe?" Her breathy voice is slightly muffled beneath the fabric.

"Don't move." I growl low and deep near her ear and watch her body momentarily tense while my fingers slip beneath her tiny sleep shorts and underpants. I slide them down below her knees then rip them off. And then I lie there, letting my eyes have their fill. Watching her breasts rise and fall with her breaths, watching the nipples tighten and pebble, her slender body quivers under my gaze.

When I can take no more, I touch her, my fingers feathering over her skin, tight and sticky from the rain. I trace long lines along her navel, up to her breasts and around her nipples. She moans and writhes under my touch. Squirms when I feather the curve of her hips and gasps when I push her thighs open. And when touching is no longer enough, I draw those same lines with my tongue, tasting the rain on her skin, watching it erupt into goosebumps each time I leave a long, languishing kiss, or suck her nipples into my mouth. Her face remains covered, and her moans are soft and needy. And then I want to take even more from her.

My fingers sink slowly between her slits. She is so wet for me I slip two fingers inside her easily, and she gasps and bucks as I do. She is so fucking beautiful all covered up and desperate and wet, and my fingers slide in and out of her till I need even more from her.

I slide down her body and push her open, and fuck she has a beautiful pussy. And though I've been inside it before, it is the first time I have taken my time to look at it. I kiss it, revering it as she moans. I taste her, and I am smitten and broken and needy. My tongue slips out and I flick her swollen clit, she mewls. I'm insatiable as I keep tasting her and my fingers rub and nudge and poke. Her legs twine about my head, her hips buck. Her body begins to quiver, and she moans. It's beautiful and I think I might break, but I remind myself that we haven't suffered enough, so I push away abruptly, grab her small waist and spin her around.

She yelps, surprised, and groans in disappointment. I know she's about to protest, but I push her head down into the sheets, silencing her. I nibble the back of her shoulders, tracing my hand along her back and across the two dimples in her hips, and I realise that this, the length of her body, is the simple answer to what I am missing, and despite that, there is still room for punishment, for desire, for suffering.

I pin her down, pushing her head further into the mattress. I don't want her moving. I help her tuck her knees below her stomach and her splendid ass is in the air on display. Her pussy glistens for me and her wild smell is intoxicating. I dip two fingers into her wetness, and she moans and pushes into me, seeking relief, but she won't get it. She's as guilty as I am.

I slide my fingers along the seam of her ass burrowing between the cheeks. She gasps, but she can't move with her head buried in the sheets. My fingers sink slowly into her ass. She whimpers, but I don't stop. I push all the way in, and this time she moans and raises her haunches, pushing towards me. Then I sink them in again, working my fingers in and out, stretching her, till she cries out in agony and despair, and then I know we are almost there, almost at the point of absolution.

I pull away one last time and crouch behind her. I am so hard and so swollen my resolve cracking under the need. She's overwhelming. I sink into her tight hot pussy in one long delicious move and slowly, I fuck her. She tightens around me, whimpering, and I pull out as we both ache in disappointment.

"Joe," she begs, but I wait, touching her, playing with her, keeping her on a tight edge before letting her fall each time. And when I have enough, I start again, pushing myself into her, and almost instantly she is rolling her hips and crying out and desperately seeking for me to give her relief. Her desperation is manic, it's like ministering to a lunatic, but again I pull out and she tenses and fights. She moans and begs, and I wait and I suffer just like her till I push into her again, and I know that this time I won't stop.

She's so hot and so ready. I thrust into her, and she cries out, her pussy clenching and sucking me in. She pushes against me and moans and screams as I pound relentlessly into her. I come hard, in long trembling jerks. I am overrun and overwhelmed by sensation. For a moment the world is a black hole that begins to disappear into itself, and then I am on the bed by her side and air fills my lungs and I am flooded with relief and delight and pleasure. There is no guilt and no anger because we suffered to get here. We suffered for our sins, and the reward was worth the punishment.

She lies above me, the corners of her eyes curled up as she smiles at me and bites my chin, playfully dragging it between her teeth. I close my arms tighter around her and pull her down so that she stops, but so that I can also still feel her body against mine, her hot sweaty skin, her breasts, her breath; all of her. But even when I am here with her, my head has wandered back to Annie. Now that the cloud of anger has passed, I think about our fight. I need to work out why she started it, what her motives were.

Amy pushes on my chest, and I'm forced to release her. She props herself on an elbow and watches me again. "You're quiet."

"I'm thinking."

"About?"

"You're young."

"So? Is that good or bad?"

"It's fucking amazing, but also it's not."

"What does that mean?"

I don't want to elaborate just now, so I divert. "I've never cheated on my wife before." At the mention of my wife her face darkens. I push away from her and sit on the edge of the bed. "I need to go."

"Already?"

I turn to her, her mouth in a sweet little pout. I shouldn't have come. I shouldn't have done this. "Things are complicated right now. My life – it's chaos."

She shuffles over, wraps her arms around my chest, and lands a sweet kiss on my shoulder. "Well, being here with you feels like mine makes sense for the first time ever."

"Don't say things like that, Amy."

"But it's the truth. It's how I feel."

"Feel?"

"Yes," she whispers in my ear, and I stand up, forcing her hands to unlatch. She falls back on the bed as I turn towards her. "I feel like I'm drowning when I'm without you."

"Amy." I search for my boxers, locate them, and put them

on. Somehow this conversation feels safer with clothes on. "You know that what we have – it's just passion – lust, right?"

"You can call it that if that makes you happy, but you know it's all about how we feel," she persists as I find my shirt and slip it over my head.

"But that's the thing, Amy. There are no feelings, there can be none. I'm married. You need to remember that."

"I'm young, I'm not stupid, and you are the one who showed up here tonight after telling me it was over between us, so don't go pretending you don't feel anything."

"Amy..." I shake my head, feeling lost.

"It's fine, go back to your family and pretend I don't exist."

At that, I launch myself back onto the bed and grab her, pulling her hands above her head, forcing her back to arch, her stomach to tighten and her face to meet mine. "But I can't."

"Can't what?" She swallows hard and licks her bottom lip.

"I can't forget you, Amy. You're totally fucking unforgettable." My lips crash into hers, the kiss hungrier than before, more frenzied and needy, and I know that I have fucked myself right up.

13

I should have stopped coming back weeks ago. Fucking Amy was meant to be a one-time thing. One night of relief, of release, and then I promised myself I'd be done.

But then I went back.

I knew I shouldn't have. I knew it. But life felt sterile and bleak. Between work, Derek's hospitalisation, and my home life, I felt like an infant being fed watered-down milk. Who can thrive on that?

Amy felt like the only good thing in my life, a place I could unburden myself – inside her – in all the ugly perverse ways Annie denied me.

Despite my brain making a million excuses not to cave in, I only ever needed one, and I clung onto it like a drunk on a railing.

So I went back again.

And again.

Until I didn't have a choice about whether or not to go back. Amy kept me feeling alive, powerful and in control of something in my life. For the first time, I knew what it felt like to be an addict. To crave, to self-medicate on lust and forbidden desire.

But then, each time I left her apartment, I was left feeling empty. Hollow. Nothing.

All I had to show for giving in to my addiction was a fading smile that dissipated as soon as I got back into my car and made my way back to my real life. That was what my life boiled down to; a routine of highs and lows. I'd fuck Amy, feed my ego and depravity and try to stay away, but it never lasted for long.

I hated the crash. The all-consuming need to go back, to touch her, smell her, feel her and come inside her warmth.

There were daily reminders of all that could be lost in the small things – each time I bathed Savannah or kissed Libby's hair, but the craving still took hold. I needed her, her body, her sweetness. It made me sick how much I wanted it and how weak I was, but still, I kept going back.

The rising sun cast a rosy hue across the morning sky. Golden fingers of sunlight clawed their way through the blue curtains, and I kiss her flat belly. She giggles, squirming beneath my touch, trying to get away from my mouth and my teeth and my obsessive need for her, but I clutch her hips and haul my body up over hers before taking her mouth, reminding her that she's mine, erasing anyone else that's come before. When we break the kiss, she pushes away and smiles. Fuck, I can't get enough of her smile, of her body, of her. I watch as she rolls off the bed and heads to the bathroom shutting the door behind her.

Even after all this time, I cannot believe that she's let me in her bed. She's so young, so perfect. Why she settled for someone like me is still a mystery, but I try not to analyse it too much. I roll onto my back and listen to the sounds of the city leak through the open window. A cool breeze makes the yellow curtain dance and lifts her scent into the air. My body shivers as I inhale her, still covered in her cum and sweat. I scrub my hands over my face and groan as I think of her bent over the couch, her boots still strapped on and her skirt inching over her ass,. The way I pushed her lacy black underwear aside and fucked her hard, fucked her like the animal I am, fucked her like the beast she allows me to be without restraints, without a collar; not like with Annie. This girl has no limits, no boundaries, and she lets me be a freer version of myself.

My cock twitches back to life as she reappears, her perfect ass on show before she bends to pick up her robe. She slips it on and ties the knot, keeping the fabric loose and most of her body on display as she makes her way to the kitchen.

"Do you want something to eat?"

"Sure," I say, pushing up on one elbow as I watch her walk out of the room again. I get up and find my boxers in the pile of clothes tangled on the floor, then pull them up and search for my phone.

Amy is spreading avocado over toast and sprinkles tomato on top as if it were cake decorations. She looks content, and for a moment I forget myself, forget what this is as I walk behind her and hug her body, snaking my hands around her waist and planting a kiss on her long neck. A subtle smile crawls on her face. She purrs as she pushes the plate across the counter. I release her, round the island and sit on the crooked bar stool that falls to the right before it settles each time I sit on it.

I watch her eat for a moment, her lips swollen and flushed, her skin glowing, the swells of her perfect fucking breasts peeking from beneath the fabric as crumbs fall on the plate.

"Stop staring." She laughs with a mouthful, and I

unlatch my eyes from her and take a bite of my toast. "How's work going?"

She changes the subject abruptly, and the whole thing feels a little too familiar, too intimate; two lovers talking about their day. But I have no intention of letting her into my life. The only place where Amy has a hold over me is the bedroom and nowhere else. "How is yours going?"

She frowns a little at my diversion. "Fine," she answers with her mouth full and swallows. "Busy."

"Is it? You rarely talk about it."

"You never talk about your work," she retorts and takes another big bite.

"You know that I can't."

"What about your family? You never talk about them either." My heart spikes at her words. There is no room for my family here.

"You never talk about yours," I throw back at her.

"Not much to say."

My gaze flicks to the framed pictures on the mantle, the smiling older couple in front of the family farm. When I look back at her with a raised eyebrow, she shrugs. I guess we've both shared about as much as we intend to.

I shove the last of my toast into my mouth and wipe away the crumbs. "I'll have to go in a minute, Annie is expecting me." She purses her lips at the mention of my wife's name.

"Already?"

"There's something I need to do. Also, tonight is our anniversary. I take her out every year, and in the morning, we'll take the girls to the zoo. It's a family tradition." My heart pangs at the thought of my family. Her face twists for a second, and I frown. Wasn't she asking about them a second ago?

"Where are you taking her?"

"We usually spend the night at a hotel."

"Of course." She huffs. "Probably some seedy hotel where you'll fuck her like a whore. Maybe like you fuck me?"

I round the counter and I'm on her in a second. She backs away from me till her back hits the fridge. I tower above her and her eyes stare defiantly into mine. There's no fear there, only challenge. "That's enough, Amy!"

"Is it? Because having you here with me just for you to go back to *her* doesn't feel like enough."

"You knew the deal when we started this. This has to be enough for you, Amy."

"Maybe I want to change the deal."

"The deal isn't up for negotiation."

"Of course, it is. All I have to do is—"

"Do what, Amy?" I stare at her beautiful face where a dark shadow passes.

"I can—"

"You will do nothing!" I growl and put my hand through her hair, grabbing her by the nape of her neck and using force to hold her there. And then I kiss her. It's a ravenous kiss at first, full of rage as I try to shut her up. She tries to resist but only a little. I rip at the robe covering her body, tug and tear at the fabric, pulling it open till it lays open around her like two broken angel wings hanging limply at her side. I kiss her again, wanting to break her apart, flay her open. I want her to yearn for me in the same way my body yearns for her. I want her to suffer. I yank her hair, jerking her head up and kiss her neck. She arches her back, trembles, but doesn't make a sound. Her silence is how she fights back.

Grabbing her shoulder, I spin her forcefully so that her back is to my front, and I push her forwards till her hips smash against the counter. I force her face onto the cold surface. Crumbs embed themselves into her skin as I pin her head there. I rip the robe from her body, and it falls at her feet. I hold her there, just watching her body shiver, watching how her back bows and her ass rises and her feet pull apart for me. Her sweet little pussy glistens. She breathes heavily and her eyes catch mine, imploring me, begging, but I ignore her.

Fisting her hair, I maintain a harsh grip as I round the counter and yank her body forward. Our plates collide with her shoulders and smash on the floor as she's splayed there, her head now hanging off the other end.

I pull out my cock, and she opens her mouth knowingly. I shove myself into her, forceful, angry. She gags, but I don't care. I want her to choke on her words, on her threats, on my violence. She swallows me whole. I give her no choice. Her eyes water and a tear leaks onto her cheek, but it's still not enough. I want to make her scream, but she can't, not with her mouth full. I pull out and away, holding onto her hair, pinning her down and round the counter once more.

I tug at her hips, and she slides backwards. I kick her feet apart then thrust once, forcefully, and she moans, losing her silent war, trembling beneath me. I stay buried inside her, deep. It's warm and soft, and my anger floods me like a tidal wave. I pull her hair, her back arches, her neck cords, her hands grip the counter, clawing at the plastic.

I pull out and haul her off the counter, spinning her around and shoving her against the wall. The breath falls from her lungs and a second tear leaks from her eye. My hands are at her ass and I lift her, crushing her against the wall. Her lips search for mine, but I deny her. She can drown in her need and anguish. Her legs wrap around my waist and her hands are like heavy chains around my neck as I press harder into her before I penetrate her. I hold us there, my hand grabbing her face, crushing her jaw, forcing her eyes to mine, as I begin to move slowly inside her. She becomes frantic, shakes her head, wants to break free, but I don't avert my gaze, and I don't release her, my hand pinching her jaw harder still.

She mouths my name, but no sound escapes, just breaths, ragged and broken.

Amy's body trembles around me. We're trapped in anger and euphoria. Her hands clutch tighter, digging into my scalp, her pussy clenching, the beginning of her pleasure building around us. She doesn't deserve to come, and I don't want to let her, but she has wrecked me, my anger overflowing into desire. I want to obliterate her, for us both to explode in lust and obsession. And then, she is consumed, screaming her pleasure, clamping down onto me, and my own pleasure forces its way out of my body as if the world has split in half and lost all meaning.

For a few moments, I hold her there pinned to the wall, catching my frayed breath, and then I leave her there, discarded against the wall and head to the shower.

The hot water cascades over my back, washing Amy and her smell away. The guilt is jaded now. That coiled snake that set itself inside my belly has slithered away, washed into the drain by hot water

The door clicks and opens, and Amy steps inside the bathroom. Our eyes meet. I'm still angry, but she's still here, she's still walking in and towards me. I enjoy that about her; her total abandon for rules. She's not like Annie with her tight legs and stern expression and the missionary position only in our bed with the occasional doggy style for a special occasion. Amy is the epitome of sex and sexiness, of intoxicating desire and freedom. She has allowed me to become an explorer, her body a new land worth discovering. Every curve and forbidden crevice belongs to me, and I mark each one, wanting to own them forever but reminding myself that this new place is only temporary, that there is already a place that is – although familiar and well chartered – nonetheless my home. And that is where I will always return.

Amy stands before me, her blonde hair falling across her breasts and her eyes roaming my body. She's noticed the weight loss, the budding muscles that have come back to life now that I've been spending time back at the gym. Annie has mentioned it as well, and I know she likes what she sees because I've noticed my wife looking at me again in a way she hasn't in a long time. Like she actually wants me. Ever since I've been fucking Amy, my relationship with Annie has flourished. Where I can come to this young girl's house and fuck her like a dog, take out all my anger and frustration on her perfect, beautiful body, it is my wife I then get to go to, and I can be soft with her, calm and collected, my thoughts already less frazzled, my body relaxed.

"I'm sorry," she says. "I don't want you angry with me, Joe."

I nod. "Don't talk about my family again." I'm stern, but I soften. This girl turns my head in all directions.

"I won't," she assures me and smiles in that shy way of hers. Except I know she's anything but, which is why it turns me on like someone has thrown a Molotov cocktail inside my body and the flames blaze inside me in an out-of-control fire. She flutters her eyelashes and takes another step towards the shower, and just like that, all is forgotten.

14

The hospital is dark and drab like my mood. Heavy grey stones and dark windows that deflect the hot sun. Despite setting Amy in her place and fucking her in the shower afterwards, I'm unsettled, and this place amplifies that feeling. It's the long white corridors and the faint smell of urine and medication, the artificial odours of chemicals that try to hide the things that keep bodies alive behind yellowing curtains.

The nurse points me towards the room and gives me a sad smile. "Wonderful news with your friend," she says, and I see the empathy and compassion in her eyes. It's totally wasted on me, but I purse my lips and give her a slight nod in thanks, hoping she buys it. "He doesn't get many visitors, you know."

I nod again. Why would he? Still, I'm both curious and cautious, so I ask, "Who comes to see him most often?"

"Just his wife." She gives me a sad smile. "She's very pretty, you know."

I don't, but I nod anyway. A tinge of guilt spirals up my spine as I wonder about his family. Then again, he gave them up when he started fucking Amy.

Each time I walk into the room I'm surprised by the amount of natural light that floods it. There's a small bedside table, on it, a small bouquet of dying flowers whose brown, wilted leaves crumble like discarded crumbs on the white surface. One floats in the glass of half-filled water on the stand. My heart beats in time with the constant beeping of the monitor, and I look at the body on the bed. My heart stutters for a second.

He's gaunt and drained of colour, and still. Just as I left him there on that grass.

Derek lies on the bed. His eyes remain closed and his breathing even. He no longer reeks of alcohol and cigarettes but of disease and desperation. A shiver runs along my back, and I take a few steps closer to the man. They told me he's woken up. The nurse said how delighted they were, but when her face dropped, she gave me a whispered apology. She said she wished there was more that could be done for my friend, but the damage is too great, that the man I used to know is probably gone.

It takes me time to set up these visits. After the weeks of rummaging through John Doe cases, searching hospital rooms and keeping my ear to the ground, finding that news article in the library gave me direction. With so many drunken losers getting beat up every weekend and ending up in hospitals it wasn't easy tracking him down, not to mention privacy laws and the fact that I can't afford to leave a trail behind that might connect me to this man at all. I wasn't entirely happy when they identified him, nor to hear he's had other visitors, but at least knowing where he is means I can keep an eye on him.

He stirs. It's the first time I've seen him move since I began to visit, and I take another step toward the bed. He moans, and for a second, I'm standing over his bloodied face in the darkness. I brush the thought away as I keep watching his face. His eyes flutter open.

The man on the bed looks at me. For a few seconds his eyes remain blank, but when he blinks again, I see recognition behind his eyes.

Derek makes a sad, desperate sound. It's small and pathetic, and I see his body shivering beneath the thin greying sheet.

"Hello, Derek." I smile at him, and his eyes bulge as he keeps staring at me. His face crumples.

I wait for him to speak, but all he can manage are a few weak sounds.

"Do you remember me?" I ask and step closer to the man. He seems paralysed inside his own head.

He keeps staring, only whimpering. His large body shakes.

"I've been coming to see you. I'm glad you're finally awake." I smile at him, and he whimpers. "I've been worried you might do something stupid when you wake up, but maybe all this time I've been worried for nothing."

I slide onto the edge of his bed, and his eyes seem to grow even more, his breath ragged and strained. I lean over him, so that my mouth hovers inches from his ear. "She's safe now, she's with me." I sit up and watch his face; something there has changed. There is no longer fear but something else I can't understand, and a pathetic groan falls from his mouth. Whatever he wants to tell me is encapsulated inside his mind, blocked by broken wires in a broken brain.

I put my hand over his, the muscles becoming rigid and hard beneath my touch. "I'll see you soon, Derek." I squeeze the limp hand far harder than is necessary. His face creases and he moans. He might be damaged, but he gets my message.

I get up and walk out of the room without a backwards look. I need to get home.

15

As I leave the hospital behind, my thoughts drift back to Amy. She's getting impatient, despite my constant reminders that I have no plans of ever leaving Annie. She knew the deal when we started. I think – not for the first time – that maybe it's time to end it with her, but the reality is, every time I'm away from her there's a yearning at the pit in my stomach that can't be filled. She's a drug that makes me feel all the things I used to feel. Young, visceral, strong, powerful.

But tonight is about me and Annie, the woman I married, the woman who brought my girls into the world and puts up with me. We promised each other for better or worse. Maybe one day soon things will be better again.

When I get home, she's waiting in the lounge, talking to the babysitter. She's wearing a short red dress that sticks to her body like rust on iron. She's not as skinny as she was when we first met, but curvy and full and lovely. The dress shows off her cleavage and black lace peaks from beyond the red fabric. Annie notices me walking in and turns. Her face breaks into a beautiful smile. She's wearing her fire engine red lipstick, or as I like to call it; blow job red. I smile back at her and watch her finish off, always attuned to the smallest of details when it comes to our girls.

"You look stunning." I kiss her on the cheek; I don't want to ruin her lipstick. I want her to ruin it on my cock later. It's the only other time in the year it's likely to happen.

"You're not too bad yourself." She nudges me with her hip and winks.

"Ready?"

"Sure."

The drive to the hotel isn't long, and Annie spends it making small talk, telling me about her day and about the girls. I spend it fantasising about stroking my wife's legs, parting them and feeling her sweet pussy as I drive. But even as I brush my fingers along her legs, she keeps her thighs closed tight and inaccessible. Not like Amy. I chase away the thought and listen, trying to be present, to be in the car with my wife instead of back in Amy's kitchen, inside her, angry and volatile and fucking insane with rage and lust.

The valet takes my car, and we are ushered into the lobby. As always, Annie gasps at the elegant grandeur. From the original grand staircase – with its striking addition of a glass elevator running up the centre – to the walnut panelling and natural light that spills into the lobby. It doesn't matter how many times we've been here, each time is like her first. I find it all over-the-top and pretentious, but Annie – she loves it, despite the fact that every year when we walk in here, she wears the same face, total awe dipped in embarrassment. I hate that she feels like she doesn't belong here, even though she's right – we can't afford this place, but once a year we deserve a night off and there is no better hotel in the city. I spend a year saving for this one night, for her, for us. It's where we spent our honeymoon, and every anniversary after that.

The first five years we had to bring Libby with us, she was just a baby and Annie's mum didn't want to spend the night with her. Now that the girls are older, we get to enjoy this more, and I don't have to spend thirty quid on some fucking chicken nuggets that only get half-eaten. I also get to fuck my wife instead of watching cartoons and waiting for a toddler to fall asleep in a five-hundred-quid-a-night room.

We check-in and I slip my hand over Annie's as I lead her to the elevator. The walls are gold plated and the carpeted floor is probably worth more than my car. We stop as smoothly as we took off and I walk out, leading Annie to our room.

When the door shuts behind us and we are alone, Annie is not her usual self. She doesn't run to the bed and jump on it sighing in pleasure as she always does. In fact, she's been quiet ever since we walked inside.

A bottle of champagne and two flutes wait for us on a table, along with a fruit basket and some posh handmade chocolates. I walk over and pop the cork. It flies across the room and the alcohol gushes from the bottle like a teenager with a porn magazine. My hand is wet and sticky, but I can't wipe it on my suit pants, they're the only ones I own.

"Would you like a drink?"

She looks at me with a strange expression on her face. When she doesn't answer, I top up both flutes. I hand her one of the glasses, we clink, and I take a small sip, noting that she doesn't. "Are you okay, Annie?"

"I need to tell you something." She looks beautiful and austere, and my heart begins to pound in my chest viciously. "Do you want to sit down?" she asks.

My stomach rolls and a slow chill makes its way up my spine. Scattered, urgent thoughts fly inside my mind as I wonder what it was that gave me away. A single strand of hair? A lipstick stain? Maybe her smell. I draw in a long stealing breath and wait for her to talk because that's the only way I'll get my answer.

"No, I'm okay." I take a long swig of the champagne, trying to wash away the sour taste that suddenly rises in my mouth.

"Well, I guess there's no other way to say it. I'm pregnant."

My heart stutters for a few beats then restarts. I'm not sure if it's relief or panic. I throw my head back, emptying the flute into my mouth with a gulp.

"Are you sure?"

Her mouth twists for a second. "Yeah, I'm pretty sure. I've taken three different tests and they've all come back positive. So I went to see the doctor two days ago, and the blood tests confirmed it." She licks her lips, her hands entwined together in front of her body, her shoulders hunched and stiff.

I clutch the back of my neck and rub the muscles even as they tense against my fingers. "How far along are you?"

"Six weeks."

I do a quick mental calculation and choke on the air in my lungs. Six weeks. The same amount of time that Izzy has been in custody, the same the amount of time I've been fucking Amy. I got my wife pregnant on the same night I fucked Amy for the first time. Guilt tries to claw its way through the walls I've raised inside myself.

My mind reels. I swallow the lump in my throat and pour more champagne, downing it. The bubbles try to burst back from my mouth, burning my throat on the way down.

I take it all in, entirely unsure how I'm feeling about it. We already had one surprise baby; the little girl who made me do the right thing by her mother. The reason I put a ring on Annie's finger. The drunken night that sees us here tonight all those years later, and now, Savannah, our baby, the one we chose to have, is at an age where she can be independent. There are no more nappies, no more toilet training, no more restless nights. Those years are behind us. They *were* behind us.

The thought of doing it all again is fucking draining, not to mention it will be another mouth to feed when we're already struggling on my fucking wage. Annie keeps staring at me, and I realise I haven't said anything for a while and that I am being an asshole. She knows I'm processing, but I know she needs something.

"Have you been feeling okay?"

"I think so." She shrugs and makes her way to the bed where she sits on the edge. "A little queasy in the mornings, but nothing like I was with Libby." A small smile ghosts her face at the memory. I'm not sure why; those first four months were fucking awful.

I study my wife, trying to work out how the fuck I missed all of this, how the fuck this could've happened. I clear my throat, realising I'm lost in thought again. "You've obviously had some time to think about this."

She nods and her eyes find mine. "This is a good thing, right? We'll be okay, right?"

I take a long breath as I hang my head on my shoulders and stare at the ceiling for a few seconds before answering. When I look back at her, I see the anxiety written all over her face. "I don't know, baby, but fuck it, we'll make it a good thing. We'll make it work. You and me."

"Can we? Really?" Her face lights up and her eyes widen, and I'm struck by how beautiful she is in this moment.

I make my way to her and sit by her side, clutching her hand in mine and holding her gaze. "I don't know if we can or can't, but you know we're going to anyway. It's our baby. We made it, and it's ours and we are going to love it no matter what. Just like we love Libby and Savannah." The words sound like an echo of something I said years ago when I bent down on one knee and thought there was still a way I could love her forever, make her happy by doing the right thing.

She bites her lower lip, and her eyes begin to glisten. "Fuck, Joe, you sure?"

Of course not, "I'm sure if you are. What do you want, Annie?"

"I want to have our baby."

"Then I'm sure."

Annie throws her arms around my neck and kisses me, hard, like she really fucking means it, like I've finally given her something that she really fucking wants. And maybe that's what she's wanted all along; just another piece of me inside her that will grow and become another tiny version of the two of us. Somebody for her to take care of, someone who will show her love, no matter what. Someone who will always need her. Maybe that's what Annie needs; to be wanted.

As I ponder these ideas, Annie straddles me, her lips attached to mine, her body grinding against me, waking me up in all the best ways. Her mouth devours mine with more heat and passion than it has for years. There's a furious hunger that she needs to sate, and it spills from her and into me as our tongues dance together and need ripples between us.

She pushes me onto the bed, and I fall backwards onto the mattress. Annie grabs my shirt and rips it open. Somewhere, a button falls with a muted thud on the ground. I can't muster the energy to be furious with her for ruining my best shirt, because she's too busy reminding me how we ended up together in the first place. She runs her hand over my chest, her nails scratching the skin, leaving behind hot trails as she pinches my nipples lightly and tugs the curly hair, eliciting a hungry hiss. Her hands make their way down and she unzips my fly. I lift off the bed, helping her to push down my pants and boxers which lock around my ankles. My cock, which is already hard and swollen, falls onto my stomach, engorged and rigid, wanting to be inside my wife.

Annie slides off me, taking her heat with her, but her eyes remain on mine. They're wild and hungry. Her hands vanish beneath the long skirt of her dress and then her black underwear slips down her legs to her ankles. She kicks out of them and mounts me again. A thrill of desire shoots through me as I see the woman I fell for; passionate, playful, as eager for me as I was for her. Her soaking pussy glides along my hard shaft and I groan, clasping her ass in my hands, forcing her movements. She doesn't protest. She takes one of my hands in hers and guides it under her dress. My fingers are immediately coated in her heat and wetness, and she moans as I set my thumb to work on her clit.

"I need you, Annie," I tell her as her eyes lock onto mine.

Annie lifts a little and uses her hand to slip me inside her. I groan at the feel of her. She's not as tight as Amy, but still soft and warm. Once she has me deep inside her, Annie begins a slow rotation of her hips. As she moves, the edges of her red dress caress my naked stomach and thighs. The curled ends of her hair bounce as she moves above me, and her mouth hangs slightly open as her breaths speed up. She's sexy as fuck as she fucks me slowly, setting our rhythm, putting us back in sync. I reach up to her shoulder and peel away the straps of her dress and bra, cupping her in my hand, pinching her nipple. Her head rolls back and she burrows her nails deeper into me. I hiss, she moans – we speed up.

"Oh, Joe." Her voice shakes as her nails tear into my chest.

"Fuck me, Annie," I say as I pound into her from below.

Annie speeds up, and I buck up to meet her, wanting to be deeper inside her. Her skin is flushed and lovely, and my thumb and thighs are soaking with her wetness. And then we are both nearly there. Annie comes a second before I do. Her pussy clenches and squeezes around my shaft, and the knot at the root of my cock dissolves into fire, and my hands dig into her ass pushing her down as I drive up. I groan as my eyes roll to the back of my head. Pleasure floods my entire body, and for a few moments we are floating, we are perfect, we are happy. I lie on the bed, wasted like a crumbling sandcastle.

Annie collapses onto the bed beside me, and I collect her into my arms, pulling her head onto my chest, letting her hair tickle my skin as we both suck in breath. I kiss the top of her head.

"I love you, Annie, I love you so fucking much." And for these few moments I really believe it.

"I love you too, Joe." And I think she does too.

We never do make it to our fancy dinner. Instead, we find each other in that room. When we check out the following morning, I know everything is different. Things need to change again, and cutting things off with Amy will have to be the first item on my to-do list.

16

"Daddy, look it's a baby." Savannah grabs my head and pushes my chin, forcing me to turn toward the giant enclosure. A baby giraffe leans its long neck toward its mother, resting its head against her silky fur and half closing its eyes. I watch my daughter looking at the creatures, completely taken and mesmerized by their elegance. She's beautiful, and watching the world through her eyes reminds me how lucky I am. How precious these moments are, how much I still have to teach her, and all the things I need to shelter her from.

"Daddy, he's looking at me. The baby is looking at me." She shrieks and waves at the animal whose rich brown eyes study my daughter as if he too was intrigued and delighted by her.

I share a smile with Annie who's has an arm around Libby's shoulder, and for a short blissful moment, the world is perfect before Libby groans and whines that she needs to go to the toilet. Annie sighs as we make a wild scramble to the nearest toilets. Out of nowhere Savannah chimes in and starts to cry stating that she can't hold it in for another second. My phone rings. It's work. I shrug at Annie who rolls her eyes and shepherds the girls towards the nearest toilet block.

I swipe the screen, recognising Sergeant Williams' number. "Hey."

"Just thought you'd want to know the lawyer is getting him out on bail."

"He's what?"

"They won't hold him."

"But—"

"I know, I just thought you'd want to know."

The line cuts off and I'm left with a silent phone in my hand. I shove it in my pocket, feeling anger rise inside me. It's like steam; it seeps from every pore and every part of me. I try to shake it off as I make my way back towards the toilet block. The zoo is full of families, kids chewing on caramel apples and cotton candy in shades of pink, yellow, and blue, sticky fingers and red lips as they get on their sugar highs and tired parents chase them around. A woman pushes a pram in front of me. She looks haggard; dark bags under her eyes as she fakes a smile at the baby she pushes. I sigh and keep walking.

As I approach, I see my girls each holding a red balloon, smiling and laughing, and Annie is talking animatedly with the seller. The girls giggle and clap about something else and then wrap themselves around the stranger. Annie pulls out her phone and indulges them as she always does. Watching their faces relaxes me a little. I feel the tension roll off my shoulders with each step, with each small giggle that pierces my heart. I take another step and reach my wife. I take her hand and kiss her on the cheek. She frowns.

"You okay?"

I nod. "Work."

"Daddy, daddy, look at my balloon." Savannah is tugging my jeans, and I find her sweet face stretched in a delightful smile. "Amy gave it to me."

I freeze. My gaze drifts away from my daughter's face and to the stranger who just took a picture with them. Amy stands with a bunch of coloured balloons. Her chequered skirt is short and covers her thin waist. She wears a black crop top that's way too revealing at the front, and subtle, natural makeup that brings out all her best features.

"Hi." She smiles at me. "You have a beautiful family." She extends her hand. "Amy."

I take her hand in mine and squeeze far harder than I need to. "Joe," I manage through gritted teeth. I can hear my blood gush around my head as my heart threatens to pound its way out of my chest.

"Nice to meet you." She smiles and pulls her hand from mine. If I hurt her she's not showing any signs of pain.

"Yeah, you too," I mumble and turn back to my girls. "Who wants ice cream?"

"Me!" my two girls scream in unison, and Annie gives me a look. It's not so much irritation as it is suspicion.

I shrug. "We're celebrating." I wink at my wife and give her a small peck, aware of Amy's eyes on us. "Take the girls to the cafeteria, I'll sort out the balloons and meet you there."

Annie smiles at me and grabs the girls. "The usual?" she asks.

"Yeah."

I watch her walk away and towards the cafeteria that I know is on the other side of the zoo.

"What's the usual?" I hear Amy behind me, and the anger that has already tickled my skin from my previous conversation flames into fury.

I whirl towards her like a tornado about to decimate everything in its path. "What the fuck were you thinking? Is this some kind of sick fucking game to you, Amy?"

"What do you mean?"

"What do I mean?" I take a few steps towards her, and she backs up toward the toilet cubicle. She stops when her back hits the speckled white wall. "Showing up here. Giving my girls balloons, taking a fucking picture with them? Are you out of your mind? Why are you doing this? Are you trying to blackmail me?" I loom over her and stare into her green eyes.

"Don't insult me, Joe."

"So, what do you want?"

"I want you to tell her, to walk away from her and be with me."

"You know that's never going to happen, Amy."

"Of course not. You'll just keep fucking me at home while you take her to fancy hotels and fuck her all night. Do you know what it was like watching you with her last night? I was going out of my mind. I couldn't sleep. Every time I closed my eyes all I saw was you and her. The way you fucked her. The way your cock was inside her instead of inside me, the way she touched your face as you came inside her."

"Did you follow us, Amy? You were watching. How?" I growl as a cold chill runs down my spine. "You've gone too far." My jaw clenches and the muscles there tense.

"I love you, Annie, I love you so much," she mimics me, panting as she does.

"Amy..."

"I need you so much, Annie." She moans, and the anger keeps rising inside me like a wild tide.

"Shut up."

"Fuck me, Annie." She repeats all the words I told my wife as she rode me on that hotel bed.

"Stop!"

"Fuck me like you—"

"Enough!" I roar, grabbing her throat and pinning her to the wall. I tower over her, our faces impossibly close. She finally stops talking, but she doesn't cower away from me. Instead, she reaches up, latching onto my shirt, grabbing it desperately like she might fall apart if she lets go.

"Do you have any fucking idea how it felt to see you with *her*, when you should have been with me?"

"This has gone too far, Amy. You need to stop." With my free hand I grab her wrists and pull them off me, but she just clutches on tighter.

"It can't stop. I *won't* stop. I love you."

"This needs to end, Amy."

"No! I've never loved anyone like I love you."

My mind reels at her words. She is totally unhinged. "You don't love me."

"I'm in love with you, Joe."

"You're fucking insane." Even as I say the word I see the devotion in her eyes, her need for me, boundless desire that I can't answer for and don't deserve. It's only been a few short weeks and she's just a kid. What the fuck have I gotten myself into?

"Don't say that. I'm in love with you and I know you love me too."

"No, Amy. Enough of this."

"Yes, please. I love you so fucking much." She keeps latching onto my shirt, tearing at it, reaching for my face and trying to find my mouth with hers.

I rip her hands away and push her shoulders, taking a step back. Her body collides with the back wall and the air flies from her lungs. The bunch of balloons rips from her hands and races towards the blue skies. "Stay away from me and my family, Amy! It's over. Do you understand me? It's over."

I leave her there as her body slides along the wall.

I don't look back.

17

"Morning, Joe." Superintendent Tom Young stands over my desk. His gaze drifts over the piles of paperwork I'm yet to get through before I start my patrol for the day.

"Sir."

"Come to my office." He walks away, leaving in his wake a tremor of uncertainty in my belly.

I close the door behind me as he sits into his well-worn, fake leather chair and brushes a hand over his tired face. He looks like a portrait gone wrong – one that the artist crumpled up and tossed away just to try and flatten out again. "Sit, please."

I sit down and get a whiff of vanilla as I do. He looks at me for a long moment with a pensive expression, and whatever hope I'd had that this would be the moment I have been waiting for and that my privileges and rank would be reinstated, leak away with his hardening stare. "Let me cut to the chase."

Fuck.

"What happened between you and Izzy, that was unfortunate, and I know you've been a good sport taking your demotion and working your ass off to make amends but" — he shifts in his chair and my heart sinks deeper— "the prosecution thinks it would be best if you were kept away from any of the Izzy files and case from now on—"

"But—"

"I know." He cuts me off with his tone and a look that demands my silence. "I know no one knows this case better or deserves the accolades. Fuck knows we're screwed and so far behind and that your help would be invaluable, but you created a fucking mess, and your name showing up on any document, any piece of evidence, anything at all, could be thrown out, so until further notice you're back off the task force."

"But, Tom—"

"There are no arguments here, Joe. It's done."

"And my rank?"

"Remains, for now."

"For how long?"

"For *now*." He doesn't elaborate and conveniently doesn't give me a timeline.

"Annie is pregnant."

"Congratulations." His smile is genuine but means nothing as he offers nothing else.

"I need to know when."

"I can't tell you that, Joe."

"I need something..."

"When I have something for you, you'll be the first to know." He stares at me with a blank expression, giving me nothing more.

"Tom." There's an edge to my voice we both hear, a dangerous anger that leaks into every part of me.

"We both have work to do. You'll be assigned a new patrol area today. See yourself out." He turns towards his computer screen, and I push myself from the chair then step towards the door. "And, Joe, pass on my congratulations to Annie."

"Yes, sir." I step out of his office, and it takes every ounce of self-control not to slam the door in my wake.

I charge down the corridor and towards the exit. Fuck this shit. Haven't I paid enough? Hasn't it been long enough? How long will I have to keep paying for a single moment of misjudgement? I barrel through the front door and into the cool air, I suck in lungful after lungful of long heavy breaths, trying to calm my hammering heart and cool the thick hot anger that coats my skin.

"Excuse me, Detective Sergeant?" I swirl at the voice and find Amy standing there watching me.

"What the fuck are you doing here? I told you, you can't come here," I whisper-hiss at her, my eyes flickering around the station.

"I know, I just..." She hangs her head for a second before looking up again. "Look, I'm sorry. I know I was out of line."

"Yeah, you were."

"It's the idea of you being with her. I went crazy."

"Keep your voice down," I hiss and take a small step back, keeping a safe distance between us. "Listen, nothing has changed, we can't see each other anymore."

She grabs my arm in desperation. "I swear, I don't want to interfere in your marriage. Your wife will never find out about us."

I shake her off and my gaze sweeps the stairway and bank of cameras no doubt capturing this moment. *Fuck.* I suck in another deep breath, clenching my fists at my sides as my gaze bores into hers. "Listen to me, Amy. Really hear me. This is over, things have changed."

"I'll do anything, Joe. Whatever you want. You can trust me." Her green eyes glisten with unshed tears and her face contorts with desperation.

"Amy. Just stop!" I pull away and attempt to step back from her again.

"Joe—I'm in love with you and I know you love me too. Look at me. Look into my eyes and tell me you don't love me."

I stare into her teary feline eyes. They're beautiful. "I don't love you, Amy. It's all in your head. Just stop now."

"You stop it, Joe! Stop treating me like this – are you telling me that all your feelings for me have changed overnight?"

"What feelings? Feelings were never part of the deal." I squeeze the bridge of my nose and look up at her. A tear escapes her eye and cleaves her cheek. "Annie is pregnant."

We stand in long silence before I break it again. "I need to get back inside."

"Please." Her shuddering breaths make her voice shake. "I'm not asking you to leave her, just don't leave *me*, Joe."

"Amy, we're done."

She wipes her eyes and sniffs, then tips her head in surrender. "Okay, Joe, we're done." She sucks in her lower lip that's tipped downwards and her eyes shimmer in the crisp morning sun. Tucking her hands into her thin cardigan, she turns away, taking the steps two at a time before vanishing around the corner.

Watching her disappear doesn't make me feel any better.

18

I had a good night's sleep. Relief is a powerful anaesthetic. Now that I have cleared the air with Amy, and Annie is pregnant and happy, things have become simpler again. There's no more lying and arguing, late-night sneaking around and leaving work for a quick blow job in the park. I have to keep telling myself I don't still want her. That her existence alone doesn't haunt me. My body misses her in ways that are profound. But I need to keep away from her. Focus on my family; she needs to understand that we're over, and so do I.

The phone on my desk rings, slicing through my thoughts. I reach for it and answer automatically. "Officer Rossi."

"Hi, Joe."

Her voice startles me, and I shoot up in my chair, my eyes slinging around the room as if she's just walked inside naked and sat on my desk. Guilt spills from the handset and coats everything I touch.

"How can I help you?" I try to keep my voice calm and professional; someone somewhere might be listening in, and of course all our calls are recorded. I run a hand over my eyes and squeeze them shut.

"I wanted to talk."

"Pretty sure I've said everything there is to say."

"Please, Joe."

"Look, Amy, I'm busy, I have to work. Don't call me again, we're done." I hang up, wiping my forehead with my wrist. It comes away wet with perspiration. I settle back into my seat as my phone rings again.

"Officer Rossi."

"Don't hang up."

I do.

My phone rings for a third time and I let my messages get it. It soon rings a fourth and fifth time, and the longer it rings, the more eyes are cast my way as the message bank blinks with its red accusing light.

The line rings again.

"Detective Rossi."

"Joe—" I hang up with my finger but keep the cradle tucked to my ear. Any calls she makes will go to my message bank, and anyone looking would think I was on a call.

I suck in a long breath. What the fuck have I gotten myself into?

I hold the phone to my ear when I feel the vibration in my pocket. The burner phone. Amy's nickname comes up on the screen, and I stare as it flashes at me before it too goes to voicemail. A missed call banner decorates my screen followed by a voicemail banner. A second later the phone rings again.

Amy has been relentless for three days. Despite my ongoing silence and brush-offs she keeps trying to reach me.

I get back to my desk after my patrol and find another message from Amy; a hand-written note left from someone at the switchboard. She's getting creative, or desperate. Either way, that's a dangerous path. I scrunch the paper in my hand and throw it in the bin.

I keep hoping the silence will push her away – will cement my decision. She's young, she has so much ahead of her, and I have Annie and the girls and so much more ahead of me. I rub the back of my neck. Another three years of nappies and sleepless nights and tantrums and Annie pushing me away, while Amy goes on to meet someone her age who will fuck her like the wild animal she is.

I grapple with my jealousy and push it out with a hard breath. She might be amazing in bed with her petite body and tight pussy, but there is enough crazy in her box for an entire asylum. I push her out of my thoughts as the phone rings again.

Fuck.

My phone is silent for the first time in five days. But I am on edge, anticipating, waiting. I don't trust the silence. And despite the cool air coming through the cracked open windows of the station, a bead of sweat meanders down the side of my face and buries itself into my stubbled chin.

I stare at the phone on my desk in wait, but still nothing happens. I push away the feeling of unease and flip through my paperwork till I am consumed by it, and for the first time in a while find escape in the black ink and greying papers. Eventually I ease myself into my seat sensing the tension fall from my shoulders. It's probably why I ignore the shadow looming over my desk. I assume it's Williams. It's always Williams. But then I get a whiff of a sweet floral scent and my head jerks up.

My eyes widen as I take her in. How the fuck did she manage to get back here? Despite the cool autumn air, she is wearing a short red skirt that rides far too high over her round ass, and a short denim jacket, faded and factory-torn in places, that hangs open showing off a black crop top that pushes up her perfect, perky tits. I tear my eyes away meeting her gaze.

When my brain regains consciousness, the anger creeps in. "What the fuck are you doing here, Amy?" I smile at her and hiss through gritted teeth.

Her ass slides along the length of my desk, forcing her tiny skirt up, exposing more of her long slender leg as she sits on the corner of it and smiles back innocently. "You weren't taking my calls." She has the decency to whisper back.

I tilt my head to the chair at the side of my desk reserved for victims or suspects, and nod towards it, too aware of the eyes around the room that leer at her and question me. I ignore them. Amy slides off my desk slowly, purposefully, driving her skirt even higher. She slips into the chair, her legs crossed tightly, a shy smile across her face.

She's fucking killing me.

Amy shifts then slowly unfolds one of her legs, setting it down a little farther than needed and holding for longer than acceptable to ensure I catch a glimpse of her sweet little pussy, taunting me with the fact she has nothing under that tiny little skirt, before crossing the other leg back over. Heat rips rough my body and goes straight to my cock, and for a minute I lose my train of thought. I swallow the lump in my throat, envisioning what it might be like to grab her by the hair, spin her around and bend her over my desk then punish her with my cock.

I lean in and her scent envelopes me making me hard and swollen at memories and fantasies. All I need to do is inch two fingers forwards and I could be inside her. I clear my throat, finding my voice as she eases into the seat. "You need to leave," I barely manage to say.

"You need to stop ignoring me."

"Fine, I'll come around tonight. Now, please leave."

"You better," she says with a sweet smile.

"Or else?" I deadpan, my hard cock deflating, my heart hammering in my chest.

"You'll be sorry. Maybe even as sorry as Derek." With that she pops out of the chair sweetly and adjusts her skirt. She leans in, giving me a full visual of her cleavage. "See you tonight, Joe."

She turns around and leaves me reeling at my desk, her ass swaying as she walks out of the station.

When she leaves the building, I bolt from my chair and rush to the bathroom, pushing my way through the door which slams against the opposite wall. I barely make it to the stall in time before I empty the contents of my stomach into the toilet. A cold sweat peppers my body and chills run up my spine. What the fuck is this girl playing at?

The rest of the day is a panicked blur. I can't concentrate on a god damn thing, and I know I'll be paying for it tomorrow with unfinished reports, late hand-ins and a fuck tonne of mistakes. But right now, there is nothing I can do about it.

I tell Annie I have to catch up on some things and will be coming home late. She's good about it. She's good about it because lately I've been good to her. I've made an effort, I've been present, I've made her feel appreciated again. I've given her a new reason to be happy.

My knock echoes through the corridor and Amy lets her door swing open a moment later. She's standing in an open lace robe that shows off lacy black lingerie. It's sexy as fuck, and on any other night I would be tearing it off her body and devouring her, but not tonight. Never again.

I push the door open, and she stumbles with a backwards step, releasing it, allowing me to step inside. "What the fuck, Amy?"

She doesn't flinch. "Hi, Joe, do you want a drink?"

"No, I don't want a fucking drink." I stalk her to the kitchen. "I want this to stop! This has to stop!"

"What are you talking about, Joe?" She takes a small sip from her glass and tilts her head with a ghosted smile.

"You know what I am talking about. The endless calls, showing up at my office, harassing me. Enough! It's fucking crazy."

"You make me sick." Her innocence falls away like a veil. "You pretend to love me, but you're a hypocrite."

"I never pretended to love you." I shake my head, dazed with disbelief.

"No, you were just happy fucking me."

"Don't play the victim with me, Amy. You came to my fucking office and threatened me. I'm not going to tell you again. Stay away from me and my family or there'll be trouble."

"Like there was trouble for Derek?" Her eyes flicker a few times, and my heart slams in my chest.

Anger slithers inside me like poison, gushing through my veins with each violent thump of my heart. I pull out my baton. "Are you threatening me, Amy?"

She looks at the baton in my hand and scoffs, her fingers lightly brushing over the metal rod.

"Amy."

"I know you want me, Joe," she says as she grabs my hand and leads the baton towards her mouth. Her lips part as she slowly sucks down on it.

I flinch away, and it leaves her mouth with a pop. She licks her lip and grabs my hand again, her mouth wrapping around the metal, my eyes locked on her lips.

Her head bobs back and forth as she takes the baton deeper into her mouth with each movement and moans as she does, her eyes locked on mine. I try to hold on to my anger, to my fear, but she is sucking it all the way down her throat with her deviance, and her soft red lips and those sexy little moans, and I can't think straight as I watch her, mesmerised by the fucked-up spectacle before me.

She pulls the baton from her mouth and licks her lips before she guides my hand. The baton traces a slick wet line down her neck, between her breasts, and down her flat stomach before she pushes it down into her underwear, and I can't help myself as I slowly push it inside her. She gasps and moans all at once, and I am rock hard as my hand starts to move of its own volition.

My other hand clinches her neck, and I push her against the wall, pinning her against it as I fuck her with my baton. Watching her eyes widen then shut, watching her mouth grimace and pout, watching her be violated by me and loving every fucking twisted minute as her body urges me on. My hand speeds up as I push inside her, fucking her hard. I want to punish her, and yet the harder I push, the more she moans, the more she urges me on. Till she whimpers and her breaths grow into harsh pants and her body arches and shakes as I bury the baton deeper inside of her.

Her moans turn to feral screams as she comes violently, her body seizing and convulsing as she tries to find more, grind more, go deeper, harder. For a few beats I stand there in awe as she unravels before me. Amy is limp in my arms as I release her and pull the baton out. It glistens with her cum. She's leaning breathless against the wall in her post orgasm euphoria, and I hate that she looks insanely sexy, and that I enjoyed her twisted little game.

"Oh, Joe." She pulls away from the wall and tries to rush me, her hands out, needing to hold on to me.

Maybe it was her voice, or her sudden movement that broke the spell, but suddenly I remember why I am here and what needs to be done. "This changes nothing, Amy. Stay away!"

I don't give her another chance to speak or protest, but I get out of there, slamming the door behind me. It's too late when I realise my baton and my hand are still covered in her cum, slick and sticky as it begins to dry.

"Fuck."

I make my way to my car and throw it on the seat. It will have to dry off. Her smell fills my car, and I pull down the windows, waiting for the cold to suck away the heat inside my body. I have never been so hard or so turned on, and no matter how fast I drive or how far I get, I can't get the image out of my head.

This changes nothing.

19

My phones have been going off again. She's filled my burner phone with messages, till the mailbox is full. She's done the same to my work phone. But I need to sit and listen to each one of her pathetic messages to ensure I don't miss something that's actually important. She whines and she threatens and she cries. She's a wreck and she leaves it all on my phone, each stage of grief as she goes through it. It's no longer insane, it's scary.

I should pity her, but I don't. I'm just waiting for her to stop. She's gone through denial and anger and bargaining and depression, so I'm hoping she accepts how things are and moves on.

When my phone flashes again, I roll my eyes and ignore the call. I wait for the message tone to blink before I listen to the message.

"Hey, call me when you can, it's urgent."

I grip my phone and call home. Annie picks up midway through the first ring. "What's wrong? Is it the baby?"

"No." She sounds annoyed. "Did you leave the fucking window in the laundry open?"

"What?" It takes me a second to work out she's talking

about a window at home, in a room I never go into. "Why the hell would I do that? I don't even go in there, and you know I don't open any windows so that the bloody cat doesn't run away."

"Well, you did, and it did, and Savannah hasn't stopped crying for two hours."

"Annie, I don't have time for this."

"Make time."

I grit my teeth and suck in a sharp breath. "What the hell do you want me to do? I have to work. I didn't leave the window open. It was probably you and your baby brain."

"Joseph."

"Look, Annie, your message said this was urgent. And obviously this isn't. I'll be home in a few hours, and we'll find the fucking cat then."

I hang up on my wife.

When I get home, Savannah is frantic. She rushes into my arms, her small face puffed and red from crying, and my heart breaks a little at the sight of her. Her distraught little face stabs my heart. "Daddy," she whimpers against my shirt, wetting it with her tears and snot, "Luna is gone." She sobs and her small hands clutch at my back, her tiny body shivering.

"Let me have a look." I pick her up in my arms and carry her around the house calling for the stupid thing. Annie gives me a dirty side look, and I still don't know why I am getting the blame for this. After a few minutes, my arms and back start to ache. I settle my daughter on the couch and promise to keep looking if she has a chocolate milk and tries to relax. Savannah puts on a brave face and agrees.

I go to the laundry room. I need to see this window. I want to prove to my wife I know nothing about it.

The window is slightly ajar, letting the cool air seep into the room.

"I've already closed it." Annie's voice cuts behind me.

"No, you didn't."

She frowns and ignores me as I fiddle with the window, shutting it again. "What the hell are we going to do?"

"It's just a cat. Relax, will you?"

Annie huffs and the muscles in her jaw dance as she glares at me. *I guess it's not just a cat.* "How could you be so reckless? You know how she loves that stupid thing."

"For fuck's sake, Annie, I never come in here. When would I have opened the fucking window? Anyway, it looks like it's broken." I point at the window that hangs open again. I frown.

I watch her brain tick over thinking about it. It's easier to blame me than the girls. I sigh, trying to breathe some calmness into the room. It's been a stressful enough week, I don't want to fight about the fucking cat. "Let me have a look at it, and then we can figure out the cat."

She nods, not entirely satisfied but clearly worried enough to go sit with the girls on the couch and comfort them.

I make my way to the window. The usually secure latch hangs slightly limp. I shut the window and lock it. It takes a few minutes, but the latch slips slowly away, and the window falls open once more. I stare at it. Then take a closer look. I pry the window open and look at the lock, finding a few tiny scratches in the wood. My heart plummets into the pit of my stomach and bile claws its way up my throat.

Fuck no.

She wouldn't dare.

Forcing my legs to take short calm strides, I make my

way to the lounge and find my three girls tucked together on the couch. The heavy feeling in my chest tightens. "Hey, I'm going to go out around the neighbourhood for a bit and see if I can find Luna. Maybe she's hiding in some bushes..."

Savannah nods, and her reddened eyes grow wide with hope. Annie mumbles something at me, but I am already halfway to the door, grabbing my keys and heading to my car.

I know I should slow down. I know I shouldn't even be doing this, but my tyres screech as I come to a halt outside her apartment building and buzz the intercom frantically.

"Hello?"

"Let me in, now!" The door buzzes, and I smash it violently against the inner wall as I push through it and take the steps two at a time to the second floor. I bang at her door, anger licking at my skin like fire, my heart like a time bomb in my chest, threatening to explode.

The door opens a fraction, and I shove it open. I think it hits her head as it does, but my sanity has trickled out of me on the way over.

"Joe, what the—" She has a hand to her forehead and her eyes are large and wild.

"Did you take it?"

"Take what?" She is playing innocent again, and my nails dig into my palms as I try to rein in my violent thoughts.

"The cat, Amy, where is the fucking cat?" Even as I ask the question, movement catches my eye and my head jerks to her window where Luna is swishing her tail, staring out into the dark street.

A small smile creeps along Amy's face. "She's beautiful, and very friendly."

"Jesus fucking Christ." I run a hand through my hair and my eyes flicker from the cat to Amy. "You broke into my house and took my daughter's cat?"

Amy takes a few steps towards the window and starts scratching Luna's head. The stupid cat purrs. "But she's safe and happy. Look how well I've taken care of her. Of course, you can take her back. I know Savannah would be so happy to see her and you'd be her hero. I basically did you a favour."

"A favour? By breaking in? By stalking my family?" I grit through clenched teeth, trying to put together the words I need to make this girl understand that nothing she did is okay. "How the fuck do you know where I live, Amy?"

I search my memories. I've been careful; always taking the train, never leaving my wallet unattended or where she could find it, a burner phone not attached to any address. She followed me and Annie to the hotel. When the fuck did she follow me home? I think about her shopping cart haphazardly filled with random items.

"You're overreacting, Joe." She takes a few steps towards me. "What you need is to relax." She reaches up to my shoulders and tries to massage my muscles.

"Get your fucking hands off me." I grab her wrists and rip her hands away then lock them in a tight grip. I drive her into the wall, shoving her hard. A garbled huff leaks from her mouth as her back connects. I pin her wrists high over her head, pulling at her shoulders, forcing her to stand on her tiptoes so that I can look into her eyes.

"You're hurting me, Joe." I ignore her, this girl that had me wrapped around her finger, this creature of my desire that is transforming into something dark and all-consuming. "If you don't let me go, I'm going to go to the cops," she whines at me.

I dip my head lower so that my lips are by her ear and my breath warms her skin. "I *am* the cops, Amy."

I pull away and look deep into her eyes, watching them grow with panic.

I push harder still on her wrists, hardening my grip till she winces. "I'm *not* going to tell you again, Amy. You need to stay away from *me* and *my family*."

Tears well in her beautiful green eyes and her voice quivers as she speaks, defeat soaking her words. "Fine. Whatever you want, Joe."

I keep her there a few beats longer, staring into her eyes, searching her face. I release her and pick up the cat. As always, the damn thing hisses at me. I have no idea how the hell I'm going to get it back home in the car without a box.

Reaching for the door I take a final look back. "Goodbye, Amy."

I don't get a reply.

When I get home, Savannah runs into my arms and snatches the poor cat which scrambles away from her and goes to hide in a small dark spot. Savannah doesn't care, and I get showered with hugs and kisses. At least Amy was right about one thing. I get to be my kid's hero tonight and my heart melts for her sweet kisses.

Annie gives me a relieved smile. Maybe I can be her hero tonight too. I pocket the thought for later as Savannah asks me to put her to bed. I take her upstairs. It's another thirty minutes by the time we finish the story about the lost cat that made it home and lights out.

I find Annie on the couch. She looks up at me and gives

me a tired smile. "Thank fuck you found it," she says as her hand flutters over her belly.

"Yeah." I fall into the couch, exhaustion dragging itself across my body. I shut my eyes.

"Where was she?"

I don't open my eyes. "She was hiding in a bush a few streets down, kept running off every time I got near her. Damn thing!" I put enough anger in my voice to convince myself, as Amy's feline eyes flash behind my eyes.

"Well, you did good." Her hand brushes over my stubbled chin, and my eyes fly open to find her close to me. "You did real good," she coos, and her mouth latches onto mine in a sweet little kiss.

I smile at her, and she leans further into me, her mouth finding mine in soft slow kisses. My arms wind around her body, tracing her long back and gentle curves. Sliding under her shirt, my hands find hot supple skin, tracing along her body in gentle practised lines. She feels good, familiar.

My hands explore, cupping her larger, firmer breasts and tickling her skin, taking my time rediscovering my wife.

When she pulls away, my lips find the nape of her neck, and I pepper kisses along the long column of her neck while she arches for me, granting me access. Her gentle breaths become heavier with each one.

Slowly, with an exaggerated tenderness, I peel the shirt from Annie, my mouth taking

a slow journey down her body, planting kisses on her skin as I work my way up and down.

I release her from her bra and underwear and take in her body, the large plump breasts, the darkening nipples, her slightly protruding belly that carries our child.

She doesn't protest as I push her onto the couch, laying her flat, pushing her legs open and admiring her pink glistening pussy. I kiss the inside of her thighs, fighting the urge to taste her. Tonight, I will be meticulous, considerate. Tonight, is the beginning all over again.

I hover over her pussy with my mouth and kiss the other thigh. She moans a little and I smile against her heated skin.

"Joe," she whispers, and I know what she wants. I know everything she needs.

I slide two fingers inside her, and her gasp is sweet and expected. Just as it always is.

I dip my fingers in and out of her soaking pussy, while my mouth still teases her skin. I crawl back above her and my mouth finds her hard nipples. I suck them in, dragging them between my teeth, eliciting a lovely moan from her.

"Please, Joe," she begs as my fingers tease and my mouth sucks. I used to love making her beg.

"Shhhhh, Annie," I whisper against her and continue my slow ministrations. Her legs begin shaking, and her back bows. She grinds against my fingers, wanting more.

I move away and stand over her, looking down at this woman I promised to share a lifetime with.

"You look beautiful, Annie." And she does, with her hair splayed across the couch and her cheeks tinted pink, her hard nipples and spread legs.

Her eyes follow the advance of my hands as I rip the shirt from my body and pull down my pants and boxers. Her eyes lock on my hard cock as it slaps against my stomach. She licks her lips and pushes up, and I stand there staring at her as she sits on the edge of the couch and her eyes find mine, begging to have me in her mouth.

I take a small step forward, uncertain. She's never been one to offer without me having to beg, but there she is, reaching for my cock and wrapping her mouth around me. I groan at the warmth of her mouth as Annie sucks the tip, working the shaft with her hands. Then slowly, with each bob of her head, taking me a little deeper. I fight the urge to lace my hands through her hair, to force myself deeper into her, relinquishing my control, allowing her to take only what she can handle. She doesn't take me deep, she never could, but her hands work me just as hard, and the sensation builds inside me. I could come in her mouth, I could coat her throat with my cum and walk away leaving her wanting, but tonight feels different.

"Stop." I pull away from Annie. "Not like this, not tonight." My voice feels tight and forced.

She falls back against the couch, and I find her mouth. I want to show her how grateful I am. I pull away and my mouth is by her ear. "Turn around, Annie." It's a strangled whisper, and I'm not sure if I'm pushing it too far, but without hesitation, she turns for me, her hands on the couch, her ass up in the air, her legs spread apart in invitation, and fuck me it is sexy as hell.

I don't wait, she's already given me permission. I slide inside her easily, slowly. Feeling her expand around me, she moans as I do, and my cock hardens inside her. Pulling out to the tip, I slide in again, feeling her shudder around me.

I keep pulling in and out, keeping an excruciatingly slow decadent pace, teasing us both, pushing us to the edge. Her body trembles beneath me.

"Please," she begs again, and she's no longer whispering. Not containing her worries.

I speed up, no longer concerned about fighting the urge. She moans for me, her face buried in the couch her ass coming up to meet each one of my strokes as skin slaps against skin. The pleasure builds inside me, and I feel her clench, her pussy sucking me in, closing around me as she lets out a broken sound. I cum hard and fast inside my wife and I am left reeling.

I collapse on top of her for a few seconds, my hands and

legs growing limp around Annie who slowly sinks to her knees.

When I find my breath, I cup Annie's face in my hands and kiss her, tenderly, passionately, like I haven't in years. She looks at me, and there is something in her face that hasn't been there before. I think it might be hope.

I lead her upstairs to bed and collapse into a dreamless stupor.

The sky is black when I leave for work. Annie is tucked into the bed, her naked body draped in our duvet and she pulls it over her shoulders, her body missing the heat of mine. She looks content, and I feel good. Last night I felt connected to her in a way that I haven't for years. The underlying resentment I'd brewed for her dissipated. Somewhere in our kisses and touches was the girl I first fancied, the girl I thought I could love forever, the girl who didn't trap me into her life with a pregnancy, but Annie, the girl from the neighbouring street with the tight ass and sweet smile and deep Yorkshire accent.

I peek in at my girls; they are sleeping safe and sound. The stupid cat lifts its head and glares at me from the end of Libby's bed, keeping my secret. I sneak out of my home and go to work.

20

My phone hasn't stopped ringing, and Amy's pursuit has become a relentless torrent of ringing and noise. It seems that the old theory of ignoring them till they'll go away isn't going to work with this one. No, this will require a more permanent and swift solution. I think about Derek.

When my phone rings, I pick up. "Hi, Amy."

"Hi, Joe, I didn't think I'd catch you today." She sounds relieved.

"Work has been busy. I'm snowed under."

"Poor Joe, you must be very stressed out."

"I am."

"Well, do you need something to help take the edge off?"

I close my eyes and let my head fall back onto my worn chair. The hot air from the heaters cradles my skin. "Maybe I do."

"Can you come over?"

"No. I don't have that much time today. I only have a short afternoon break."

"Aww." There's a chink in her confidence.

"But maybe you can meet me at that spot at Regents?"

I can almost hear the smile spreading across her face. "Yes, it's been a while since we've been there."

It has. Almost three weeks by my count; long enough for the sweltering summer heat to die down and for autumn to set its clutches into the city. "It has. I'll see you there at four."

"Can't wait."

"Me either." I hang up leaving her with that.

Four p.m. is not an ideal time to try to commit a brutal assault, but the fucking girl has left me no choice. If I tell her to meet me at Regents for a blow job at midnight she might get suspicious.

Despite my plans to bludgeon her over the head and leave her for dead, my cock hardens at the thought of Amy on her knees, watching as my cock vanishes inside her warm, wet mouth, listening to her hungry moans as she swallows me again and again, her feline eyes glued to mine as my hand fists her hair.

I shift in my chair and try to concentrate on the paperwork in front of me knowing I won't be able to. Parts of me don't care anymore. With Amy running around like a loose cannon, Izzy out on bail, and work basically shafting me up the arse without a timeline for when I'd have paid my dues, I've run out of fucks to give. At least this afternoon I will take care of one problem. Maybe it will have a domino effect and once Amy is taken care of the rest will all fall into place. With that thought in mind, I go to the toilet and deal with my hard on.

The cap sits low over my face as it always has. Amy won't get suspicious. Even on our previous meets I've always attempted to hide myself as much as possible. I can never take the chance of being recognised, and today is no different.

I lean against the old oak tree, standing in the shadow it casts over the perfectly manicured lawn. It hides amongst a row of other oak trees, and if I stand in just the right spot, I am invisible to anyone on the path or that might come around from the grassy lane behind.

Amy is wearing a long dark trench coat that falls halfway down her calves, and her hair is made in two braids that bounce over her shoulders. I know she can't see me as she approaches, but as always, I am entranced by her. Looking at her is like staring directly into the sun; the intensity of it burns and yet you can't stop.

She looks about a little as she moves off the path and makes her way to me. When she catches a glimpse of me, her face splits into a lovely smile. She speeds up a little, as if unsure I'll still be here if she takes too long. I don't move.

"Joe." She leaps on me. Her tongue is inside my mouth, her hands are in my hair, and her wild scent fills me up. I push her away, breaking the kiss.

"Hi, Amy. I don't have much time." Her gaze slips down to my hands where I unzip my pants. Her tongue slips out of her mouth and licks her bottom lip, and in an instant I'm hard.

Without hesitation, she falls to her knees and her hands get to work on my boxers, releasing my cock. A second later I am inside her mouth and the perfectly constructed plan I had begins to vanish.

Fuck.

She sucks me lavishly into her mouth like my cock is decadent chocolate, and the way she purrs around my tip as it hits the back of her throat makes me harder. My hands grab her braids and I start to work her head, losing track, losing my grip. This isn't the reason we're here. I yank her head violently and fall from her mouth. Pulling hard on her hair, I force her to stand. She moans a little but doesn't resist. She's the perfect victim. A willing one.

I smash her back against the tree, and then I'm on her. She's expecting me to fuck her, not to choke her, and I expect no resistance. But that's my mistake. My head is too foggy with the memory of her lips on my cock. It swings around between us, the cool wind sucking the heat from it, sobering me up.

"What are you doing?" she gasps as my hands constrict tighter around her neck, the sexy pink hue of her cheek turning a dark crimson.

"This has to stop, Amy." My grip tightens, and she tries to gasp for air, her muted gulp urges me on, and my fingers close around her oesophagus. A quiet exit. Draw no attention to ourselves; no screaming, no mess. That will come later.

"Joe?" Her eyes begin to bulge and red floods her face as I tighten my grip further, and Amy realises what my intentions are. I don't think she ever gave real thought to how far I am willing to go to protect the ones I love, like my mother and Annie and the girls, and even her I protected her – maybe she never knew how far I went. Or maybe she did.

She starts to struggle. Her hands come to her throat and she pulls at my fingers, trying to pry them off, but I tighten my grip. My heart thunders in my chest, violently ripping my insides. She wheezes and gurgles, the muscles vibrating under the force of my grip. The fight seeps out of her quickly.

In a last-ditch effort she slashes at me. Her nails rip into my neck taking some of my skin with them. "Fuck!" Sweat pours into the small nicks and stings. Now she has my DNA under her fingernails. The minute distraction has me releasing my grip slightly on her, she seizes the chance, kicking me full in the groin where my floppy dick still hangs in the cold.

I crumble.

I roll on the ground, clutching my cock as white pain burns inside my body, slashing its way up my spine and to the back of my eyelids. I groan and try to find air in my collapsing lungs. Amy bends over and sucks in deep breaths. She gags on air and dry retches, clinging desperately to the tree. Her gaze falls on my face, her eyes full of questions.

She sucks in another lungful of air. "What are you doing, Joe? That's not funny." Her voice is tainted with betrayal.

"It's over, Amy," I spit out in my hoarse voice, shaking in pain and rage. I can't believe how badly I've managed to fuck this up. "We're done."

She glares at me, her eyes burning into mine before she straightens up, closing her trench coat. "I thought you were different, Joe, but you're all the fucking same," she hisses. "You want me to stay away? You want us to be over? Fine! I can't wait to forget about you and wish I'd never met you." She sneers then leaves me there like a turtle on his back.

Fuck.

Anxiety chokes me. It fills up every part of me like smoke as I wonder where the hell she's vanished to. I stop over at her apartment, but buzzing the bell achieves nothing. All my texts go unanswered, as do my phone calls. My mind chugs back to the way her eyes grew large, slowly popping out of their sockets, her cheeks flooded with dark angry red.

I drive past the house. Annie's car is in the driveway and

the lights are on. I park my car out of sight down a side street and scour the house, searching for foreign movement.

I should have fixed that fucking window.

I lose track of time and my phone starts to buzz in my pocket. It's the chief inspector. He never fucking calls. I ignore it, but it rings again and then a third time.

I get back in my car and hightail it to the fucking station.

I am a dog with its tail between his legs, castigated and put to shame. There was no lying to Tom. My GPS put me where I shouldn't have been and all my excuses were lame at best and pathetic at worst. At least he did me the courtesy of sitting through them. When he asked why I was bleeding, my hand flew to my neck, and I started a new string of lies. He stopped me, midway putting us both out of our misery.

Another talking to, another shake of the head, another black mark against my name.

The rest of my shift drags like a wounded snake pulling itself along a blazing road, and my anxiety runs my imagination like a motor. With each passing minute my nerves feel flayed and raw. There is no calmness, not while I don't have any idea where she might be. I've been chained to my desk, no more patrol for me, only the station where I can be watched, like a child. Resentment takes its seat as a passenger to my dread.

I stare at the paper folders piled on my desk and think about Amy. "Fuck," I say a little too loudly. I ignore the room and pick up a file, flipping it open at random. I stare at the page seeing nothing but my mistakes, my incompetence, and my teeth grind. My jaw aches with tension, and I bolt up, earning myself a few more looks. I sit back down, my hands gripping the arms of my chair, and all I want to do is rip them off and throw them at something.

I suck in deep breaths, reassuring myself, trying to convince myself that everything will be okay. All I have to do is find her, talk to her. She'll understand. My body begins to believe my lies. The strain in my muscles dissolves and my grip softens. Until I close my eyes and see hers – angry and full of betrayal. I stand up, unable to ruminate in my seat any longer. Williams tracks my movements as I walk to the men's room.

Leaning over the sink, I stare at myself in the mirror. My neck burns with the red scratch marks as it cords. "You fucking idiot," I hiss at the reflection, then push off the sink and begin to pace the small space. Thoughts whirl inside my head like a savage tornado. I shake my head, trying to shake the thoughts away, but they persist. I suck in a few breaths and remind myself that I am a policeman. I am smarter and older than her. I have resources, and even though I can't leave the station while on duty, I'm sure there are ways I can find her. I could go down to the IT department; Chris still owes me a favour. Maybe he can find her phone, give me a location.

I keep pacing, every step bringing more clarity, more calmness. Until it doesn't. Until the room begins to feel too small and the air too thick and my lungs feel inadequate to hold any air, and I realise that even Chris can't bypass the tracking and logs. "Fuck." I growl into the empty room and find my reflection in the mirror. I glare. I stomp over to the sink, my eyes burning, my muscles tense. The angry beast holding me captive takes control of my entire being, and before I can help myself, I smash my fist into the mirror. The air is rent by the sound of fracturing glass. It holds together, and I stare at the multitude of eyes that stare back from the splintered mirror, my heart jackhammering inside my rib cage. "Fuck," I whisper as I cradle my throbbing fist and walk back to my desk.

At the end of my shift, I bolt from my chair and rush to my car. If the chief saw me reckless driving, I would likely be suspended for good. I don't care. My body trembles as I drive, my uncertainty becoming a tangible, living force that creeps over me like some hungry beast, gnawing at my core.

I slam the car door and rush inside. Annie gives me a sideways glance, her eyes momentarily settle on my neck, but the girls – having heard the door – come rushing towards me. I hold them in my arms as my gaze sweeps the kitchen. Everything is just the same, normal, and that makes everything somehow worse.

I jitter through dinner and ignore my wife through the movie she picked, deflecting her questions about my injuries, putting it down to a violent arrest. She remains silent, but her eyes sting with disbelief. My gaze constantly flicks to the front door or the back of the house. If Annie notices, she says nothing. I spend the night tossing and turning, listening to my pulse beating in my ears, blocking out every other sound.

21

The morning is a tired haze of heavy limbs and scratchy eyes. I don't want to be awake, though I'm not entirely sure I slept at all. For a few seconds, I try to convince myself that yesterday was a nightmare, but when I grab my razor and shave my thick stubble, the hot water runs into the recent furrows Amy left behind and burns.

Fuck.

I drive to work. The sky is like an ocean that's gone still. Everything feels wrong.

My stomach churns slowly, like it's moving dry cement in my bowels. My insides hurt and my eyes keep flickering to the clock. I spend most of the day watching the shadows moving across the floor and the web at the back of Ben's chair. It's abandoned now, just a few old strings hanging onto the fabric pulled down by gravity. I can relate.

Each time I look up, I catch the eyes that turn away from me. They all keep staring. The same thing happened last time too, after I got reprimanded, after I got told to sit down in the corner and wait for my punishment – a mixture of awe and disgust. Now all I see is pity. Fuck them. I don't need pity. I just need to get home. I don't trust Amy's silence.

There is something familiar in loud anger. It resonates. It's violence and frustration and once out it dissipates into the world. But silent anger, that is by far more concerning. It is insidious and calculating and hidden behind a sweet face.

The cement hardens inside me.

As soon as I get home, I know something is wrong. It's silent. No blaring TV in the background, no screaming girls, just my wife and a half-drunk bottle of wine.

"What the fuck do you think you're doing?" I reach for the bottle, but she snaps it away, the kitchen bench an island between us.

I look around. "Where are the girls—?"

"Who the fuck is Amy?" A pit opens at the bottom of my stomach and my heart starts to fall. It keeps falling into a dark, empty abyss as the question hangs between us.

"Annie."

"Who is she?"

I wipe my hands on my jeans. "Where did you hear that name?"

"She dropped in. Invited herself for a cup of tea. Imagine my surprise that the girl who gave my girls balloons at the zoo and took a fucking picture with them has been fucking my husband." Her face twists in a grimace. "She asked me to send you her love." She scoffs at the words.

A cold wave embalms me as the hairs rise on the back of my neck and my mouth runs dry. "Annie..."

"How long?"

"Annie—"

"How long have you been fucking her?"

"Annie, don't."

"How. Long?" She shouts, and I look behind me at the stairs. Annie doesn't take her eyes off me.

"A few weeks."

"Weeks?"

I don't answer.

"Do you think she's prettier than me?"

"Annie."

"Do you?"

I sigh. It's long and heavy and I look into my wife's drained face. "I think she is pretty."

"And younger?"

"Annie."

"Is that how you like them now?"

"Don't."

She scoffs at my veiled threat and takes another sip of wine. My eyes snap to her belly, but she ignores me. "Is she better than me?"

"Annie, please—"

"Fuck you, Joe. I asked you a question. Is she better than me?"

I pull at my shirt as if it's suddenly too tight, the fabric suffocating. "Not better, only... different."

"How?"

"Annie—"

"How?" She raises her voice again and her face is stone cold, frozen in devastation.

I swipe my forehead and run a hand along my mouth, dragging it slowly down. "She's more... open to things."

"Open to *things*?"

"Yes."

"Did she suck your cock?"

"How is knowing that going to change anything?"

"Just answer the Goddamn question!"

I look away from Annie and sigh, then back at her face, pleading with my eyes, but she doesn't budge. "Yes."

"Did you fuck her in the ass?"

"Yes."

"Did you make her come?"

"Yes."

A slow silence settles between us like a deadly frost. Brittle and harsh and frigid.

"Annie—"

"Don't!" She raises a hand and stands, tears welling in her eyes, tears she won't shed in front of me. "Get out."

"Annie—"

"Get. The. Fuck. Out. Of. *My*. House." She enunciates each word as she spits them out.

In an instant our years together are erased. Even as I try to convince my wife that she is overreacting, that there is a way past this, a way for us to survive – she only keeps telling me to leave. There are no more words, and as I close the door behind me and fall into my car seat, reality hits me like an anchor.

I've lost Annie. I've lost my girls. I've destroyed my family.

I know her well. Despite our differences, we'd lived together for years. She is a fortress. When she lets you in, you are safe and warm, all your needs are catered for, but most importantly, you have her trust. But once that is broken, she will throw you out and put up barriers, and you will *never* regain entry. Not after this. I realise as my back sticks to the seat that all we have built is nothing but dust at my feet. All our future plans are erased.

I smash my palms against the steering wheel, cursing every god in the fucking universe, blaming everyone but myself. I did everything right. I saved her. I helped her. I kept things a secret and she was the one that spilt it.

Fucking Amy.

I sit in my car watching my house, watching as the lights go out and my heart, just like my house, becomes engulfed in darkness.

When my phone rings, the shrill tone cuts through the ugly silence and Amy's name flashes on the screen. That little bitch has the audacity to call me. I stare at the name, the screen bright in the darkness. My hand clutches the phone, but I don't pick up. Not the second or third time either.

When she calls for the fourth time, I pick up. "What the fuck did you do? You ruined my marriage, my fucking life."

"I'm ending things, just like you wanted, Joe."

"What the fuck does that mean?" My knuckles blanch as my grip tightens around the phone and the line cuts away on the other end. "Amy? Amy?" I shout her name into the silent phone.

I call her back, but she doesn't answer. I try a second and third time, but the line just rings out.

"Fuck!" I pull and tug on my steering wheel like a mad man, then crank the engine, pulling away like a demon. I drive too fast and too recklessly as I plough my way through the dark streets and towards her apartment.

My tyres screech as I come to a stop and park unevenly, the butt of my car jutting out of the perfectly straight line. I don't give a shit. Slamming my car door, I rush towards her apartment building and ring the buzzer. She ignores me. I buzz again, holding it in for longer, and still, she ignores me.

"Amy." I call her name and bang on the door, buzzing her apartment. "Amy!" I scream again, feeling the anger rise inside me like smoke; dark, thick and suffocating. "Amy!" I call again, banging and buzzing, and still she doesn't come. Above me, the apartment building lights up like a Christmas tree as every tenant hears me below them.

The lobby explodes with light, and there, on the other side of the glass door appears Amy. She is wearing a loose white singlet and short pyjama pants and is holding her phone. She walks towards me, long sure strides. She smiles at me. It's one of her beautiful ones, one that could melt an iceberg with its intensity. And as I stop and stare, her face creases and folds, her smile crumples, and tears begin to leak down her face. I see terror there, ugly and fierce and unwarranted. Her phone appears in her hand. She holds it up and dials, making sure I see the numbers.

999

She puts the phone to her ear, and a few seconds later she starts to speak. I retreat from her door, and she watches me take a few startled steps back. As she talks, her face changes again, and she winks at me.

I bolt to my car and drive away.

Morning comes in streaks of light blue that carve through the black curtain as if it has been clawed by a beast. My body aches and my eyes burn as I push myself out of my car and stare at my front door, knowing somewhere behind it, Annie is likely waking up to an empty bed and getting my girls ready for their day. My life feels immediately emptier without them.

I take a few stiff steps and knock on the door. She makes me wait. I don't blame her. When she finally comes to the door, she is almost unrecognisable. Her beautiful blue eyes are puffy and red, her complexion stark and pale, and her face drawn and miserable. Guilt stabs at my heart with its sharp claws, knowing I am the one who caused this.

"Annie, can I come in please?"

"No."

"Annie—" Tears pool in her eyes, and I want to look away from the devastation I've caused, but I don't dare take my eyes off her. "Please?"

She wipes her eyes and straightens her back, pulling her robe tighter around her. Her voice shakes when she speaks. "After I drop the girls off, I'm going to call a lawyer. I'm going to take everything; the house, your money, our girls, you will never see this baby!"

"Annie—"

"No! I've stood by you. While you didn't come home, while you fucked up your job, while you fucked some little girl instead of coming home to us. You made your choice, and I've made mine. I've earned this. You owe me."

I stare at my wife. This woman with whom I've shared my bed for almost thirteen years, and what I find is a cold-hearted stranger. "I *owe* you? What the fuck, Annie? This is a marriage. For better or worse."

"Pfftt. We both know that if you'd used a condom that night neither of us would be here."

I glare at my wife. We both know it's the truth, but it's always remained unspoken.

"You crossed the line, Joe. There's no coming back from this."

"Annie." I try to reach for her, but she flinches back, hiding her body behind the door.

"I need to get the girls ready." She closes the door in my face, and I hear the lock click into place.

Fuck.

22

Staring at my reflection in the rear-view mirror, I brush my fingers through my hair, attempting to tame the wild strands. It's not working. I look tired and haggard and my shirt smells – the sweat dried in the pits staining a faint yellow. There's not much I can do about it now. I have a spare uniform in my locker.

I walk into the station, sticking to the walls, attempting to remain invisible. I need to make it through this day, collect my thoughts and find a place to sleep tonight. But even as I try to escape to the bathroom, Williams is there. He looks me up and down. There is something like contempt in his eyes. Or maybe it's disgust. The judgement irks me. Has he looked at himself lately?

"You look like shit."

"Maybe I'm a mirror."

He scoffs, but barely. "Tom needs to see you in his office."

"Tell him I'll be right there." I try to sidestep him, but he steps with me, blocking my way.

"It's urgent."

"It's never urgent." I try to step again, but he doesn't budge.

"This time it is." His face is set, all the soft roundness gone, replaced by angry edges.

I sag as the last of my resilience leaves my body. "Okay, let's go."

Tom doesn't offer me a seat as I walk in. His eyes narrow, his expression solemn, his mouth carved into a tight line across his face. Williams doesn't leave the room. I watch him over my shoulder. He's blocking the door.

"You wanted to see me?"

He nods; it's curt and cold and unlike him at all. "Someone has come forward."

A chill runs through me as I wonder which of my recent misdeeds has been noticed. I know it's not Derek. He is still tucked into his bed at the hospital, his memory all but wisps of smoke. I remain quiet and still. When I don't speak for a few beats, he shifts in his seat as if he's disappointed I haven't given a full confession. The thing is, I don't know which of my crimes he wants me to confess to.

"The charges are serious, and I am afraid that given the grievous nature of the accusation, I am going to have to suspend you – with pay – for now – until we get it all sorted out."

"What are you talking about? What charges?"

"You will need to hand in your ID, radio, baton and car keys."

"Tom—"

"Don't make this more difficult than it has to be." Williams takes a small step forward behind me. I don't see it, so much as sense it. His shadow is large and dark and closes around me.

"What are the charges?"

"Your things, Sergeant." His voice is formal and sharp,

any friendliness that might once have been there has vanished.

I rip my ID from my top pocket and pull out the baton from my belt, setting both on his table. Next, I fish my keys from my pocket and fling them down. They land with a heavy clank. "How the fuck am I meant to get home?" But as the words leave my mouth it fills with a sour taste that curdles my gut. *I have no home.*

"It will be a few hours until we finish the inquiry. I'm sure one of the boys will drop you at your home when we're done."

Williams doesn't volunteer.

The chief eyes my things and picks up his phone. He dials an extension and we wait in silence. "Come in." he speaks to the voice on the other end of the line and hangs up abruptly.

A few minutes later there's a knock at the door and one of the lab geeks walks in. He doesn't greet me. He's wearing gloves and has an evidence bag in his hand. Reaching for my baton, he secures it in the bag. Tom hands him my keys. "The car is parked outside, unit 23." He nods and leaves without another word. A trickle of panic quivers inside me.

"She's lying." I slip up and bite my tongue. Tom's eyes snap to mine and his shoulders square.

"Don't say anything more," he warns me and nods towards Williams, who comes to stand closer again.

"Williams here will escort you to interview room five."

"I don't need an escort, I know where it is."

"I think you will find that you do." Muscles jump along his jaw as his hands steeple in front of his face and his eyes lock on mine. In them, I find a well of disappointment. "It's a shame it's come to this. I had such high hopes for you."

With that, he breaks eye contact and simply nods at

Williams, who steps aside, opening the door for me. "This way."

I shoot him an irritated look. "I know where we're going."

"You're lucky you're not in handcuffs," he hisses, and his words are shards of ice that embed themselves under my skin.

Walking through the main room, I feel every set of eyes on me. They burn with anger and hatred. I hear the whispers. They are like maggots crawling inside me; I can feel them, but I can't reach them. I can't make them stop.

We turn left at the corridor, towards the narrowing hallway where the interview room awaits. As we approach room number five, the door to room number four opens and a female officer I've never seen before steps out, holding the door slightly ajar. I look to my right as we pass and see Amy. Her face is tear-streaked, her eyes puffy, her neck a shade of ugly purple and a forensic technician is scraping under her nails. My hand shoots to my neck as the man meticulously collects my DNA from her.

Her eyes flicker up and she notices me. She feigns terror. Her hand shoots up to her neck as her eyes grow wide and round, and the officer in the room with her looks up to see me. Rage erupts inside me like venom, cold and menacing, poisoning my insides, infecting every cell and nerve, bleeding into my bones and bleaching my skin. Till all that is left is pure, unadulterated hatred.

"What the fuck did you do, you stupid bitch?" I scream at her and lunge, but Williams throws his arms around me, and the female officer slams the door shut. I hear the latch set in place and panicked words exchanged inside.

Two officers I've never seen before rush out of the next room and haul me into number five before pushing me down into the chair. They introduce themselves as officers of the independent office for police complaints and tell me to calm down.

"You calm down! She's lying! You have no idea how fucking crazy she is." I eye them like a crazed animal, my heart smashing against my ribs.

"Why don't you tell me," the officer I've never seen before says as he sits calmly on the other side of the table.

The next few hours are a blur. They keep asking me questions about how we got together, about why I was seen at her apartment banging like a crazed man at her door and about my baton covered in her bodily fluids. A forensic technician takes swabs and DNA samples, a photographer takes pictures of my neck and torso. I want to break everything.

I try to explain. I need to dig myself out of the hole she has somehow buried me under, but the more I talk, the more I tie myself up in knots.

I tell them this isn't the first time this has happened, that she's a manipulative shrew, and they ask if anyone can corroborate my story. I shake my head furiously, thinking of Derek in that fucking bed drooling and pissing into a nappy, and I know she's covered all her tracks and I am fucked.

23

EIGHT MONTHS LATER.

The hospice is deserted. A dirty, derelict building where bodies are kept alive by machines and medicines. Still smells like piss.

I sneak into his room, the cap lowered over my face. Not that it matters. I've become unrecognisable. By the time I close the distance from the door to his bed, the guilt has eaten me like vultures ravish a corpse. I push it aside.

He's lying on the bed. His face has sunken in since the last time I saw him. It's because most of his food comes through a fucking tube. The room is dark and dreary, like the clouds outside have somehow congregated inside his room. I step closer to the bed, and he flinches. He knows I'm here.

"Hi, Derek." I sit in the chair next to the bed. It's too soft and I sink into it. He tilts his head to the right and opens his eyes. He barely reacts.

I sigh, looking at the man I crippled. He's stayed just the way I left him – broken and alone.

"I... um..." I stammer, the words lodging in my throat. Talking to him here would be an admission, but I've done so much wrong I need to do this. Maybe part of my conscience can still survive.

"I'm sorry." I blurt it out, and his eyes open a fraction more. I scrub both hands over my face as I search for the right words. "I didn't realise what you were doing. I should have listened."

There's a muted rasp as he opens his mouth, and I think he wants to speak. I push forward from my seat, searching his face. His lips twist and a broken cackle breaches his dry lips. It's sharp and hoarse. I search his face as I straighten up and move away from him.

The cackle grows, trickling out of him in a maddening cascade that turns into a hysterical ugly howl. It's harsh and throaty, and he begins to choke on his laughter. His body shakes on the bed like he might be having a fit, and still his contorted face twists as the cracked laughter falls from him and fills the room.

I back away. His body folds in on itself and he coughs like a dying man, spurting and moaning, but still he laughs, his mad eyes glued to my face.

I retreat from the room, the laughter following me like a dark shadow all the way to the elevator.

I lurk outside the house, the one that used to be mine. I'm across the street, hidden in the shadows. If I breach my restraining order, they will throw me back in jail. Anger flickers inside me as I think about it all. I watch Annie as she drives up to the house. She's smiling as she lets the girls out of the car. They are all talking animatedly, laughing, having fun, as if I was never a part of their lives, as if I wasn't viciously sliced out and thrown away like a rotten piece of meat.

Annie opens the back door and pulls out the baby carrier. My son is asleep, totally unaware of my existence. The girls rush their mother and new sibling, cooing and reaching out. My fists clench, my dirty nails digging into my palm. I don't even know his name. She didn't even let me know when she went into labour. All I got was a text and a blurry picture two days later. The rage slices my insides, threatening to burst, and I clench my jaw forcing it down.

I want to hold my son. To smell the top of his head and make him empty promises about how good life is going to be for him. But I can't. She won't let me near him. She won't let me near any of them. Of course, I could fight, drag it out, make her pay, but she seems so goddamn happy. They all do. I've broken enough things. Somewhere inside of me, a longing flares – a desire to go back, to change it to how it used to be, to get my life back. But it's as futile as my rage.

The girls walk inside and lights come on in various rooms. In my mind's eye I see Annie going into the kitchen to start preparing tea while the girls run to the lounge or their rooms to play. She'll feed the baby and they will have turns holding him. They giggle and laugh and ask when Daddy is coming home. I let out a ragged sigh.

The ache in my chest returns, like a heavy stone has been placed on it and it gets heavier each day. Heavier to carry, heavier to breathe. When I asked to see the girls, Annie insisted the visitations be monitored, like I'm some kind of feral dog that would hurt our babies. She never talks to me, not directly, just through her lawyers. The last time I approached her for a conversation she had me arrested for breaching the restraining order she put out on me. She put the kids under its protection too. I can't go near my babies. My heart tips.

I stay a little longer, knowing that once that door closes

nothing more will happen and there will be no more glimpses, just dreams.

I pull out the brown paper bag holding my bottle of whiskey and take a slow swig. The liquid burns everything inside. I want it to erase everything. By the time I finish the bottle it will.

I walk around aimlessly. The streets are quiet. Most people are gathered inside, huddled together, keeping away from the vicious cold. I make my way to the tube station. There's warmth down there but also a cacophony of sound and lights and humanity. It makes me feel like I'm home for a while; the noise, the laughter. Of course, no one sees me. I've become invisible, no longer in my uniform but my week-old clothes needing a wash, the stubbled unshaven jaw and the gaunt, drawn eyes. I'm tired.

Some days I sleep at the halfway house. Everyone keeps to themselves. Everyone has a past they want to forget. Everyone is trying to rebuild something they've lost. My only reprieve is that the departments agreed to keep my arrest and consequent deal out of the media. It was still a shit show; someone got wind of it all and they were out for my blood. Dirty cop, dirty allegations. The system is always under so much scrutiny, being looked at by the outside through a magnifying glass, but they swept it all under the carpet. They didn't want Izzy's case affected. My name was still attached to too much paperwork. We were forever entwined in each other's lives. In the end, it didn't even matter. Not even when the charges were dropped, when she pulled back. By then my name was tainted, my reputation in tatters, my life unrecognisable. The city paid me out, but Annie wants to take that too. I take another sip of my whiskey and get on the tube.

It smells like urine and desperation, or maybe I'm just

smelling myself. It rattles beneath me as we rush through tunnels and stations.

Light.

Dark.

Light.

Dark.

There's a young couple a few seats ahead. The way she looks at him is the way Annie used to look at me; with desire and delight. The way he looks at her is the same way I looked at Amy; lust and ferocity. He runs his hands along her long legs, and she lets him. She giggles, he kisses her neck. I look away.

I get off at the next station.

The young couple gets off at the same stop. The boy eyes me with suspicion and they give me a wide berth. When the hell did I become the bad guy?

I have a sudden and desperate need to get away from the manufactured lights and thick stone walls, and I rush up the stairs. Somewhere below me, the couple laughs; at me or with each other, it doesn't matter.

I find myself in familiar territory. I didn't mean to come here, but somehow, I ended up here again – like I often do. I don't know why. Despite everything that's happened, I still come here. I'm like an addict in search of my dealer, the one that has the best product, the most poisonous, the most devastating.

I stand outside the Seven Eleven. The harsh light from inside falls across the tarmac like broken sunshine. I gulp at my whiskey. I've almost had enough to make another day vanish like the harsh vapours when I spot her. I do a double-take and blink through the haze, but it's her.

Amy has her hair up in a tight ponytail and her hair swishes across her shoulders. She's wearing a tight, fake leather jacket and one of her signature skirts. Her leggings are ripped in places, showing off bits of skin before they sink into her boots. She's holding two bags of groceries and she looks so fucking content – like everything is fucking perfect.

I tear across the road like a demon and cut off her path, startling her. "Amy," I growl.

She stops dead for a second, her eyes large and her face drawn. She searches my face and then hers seems to fall back into place as she recognises me.

"Joe." She smiles at me. *Fucking smiles*. "How are you?"

Anger slithers inside me like a burning snake and it scratches my insides. The fire fuelled by the alcohol sets a maddening rage beneath my skin. I grab her elbow and pull her away from the light and into the nearby alley where we can have some privacy.

I push her against the wall, and she huffs a little. She's still smiling at me. I lock a hand around her wrist and push it up against the wall, pinning her there.

"How am I?" I move in closer to her, my face inches from hers. I can smell her wild scent over my own, and my body remembers all the things I wish it never knew. "You ruined my life," I growl at her.

"You were the one who wanted to end things, but it's not too late." Her hand reaches for my face, and I flinch away.

"You're fucking crazy—"

"Miss, are you okay?" a voice interrupts us.

My eyes flicker over to the intruder. A police officer is standing just outside the alley. He is about my height, clean-shaven and neat. My eyes go back to Amy's. "She's fine. It's you who should be careful."

"Step away from her, sir," he says, and I sigh as I release Amy and take a small step back from her. I'm not the dangerous one here. He needs to read the situation better and take my advice. "Now move along." He's trying to get me to leave, but he doesn't understand. He needs to save himself.

I turn to the police officer. "Walk away while you still can."

"Sir, I think you'll find you're the one who needs to walk away." I know he'd rather I leave. I know he has no interest in arresting some drunk fuck and spending his night doing paperwork.

"Look, I'm warning yo—"

"Don't threaten me." He reaches for his baton and his body tenses. I think through my options. I can get arrested and save this idiot the heartache, but that would mean I'd need to involve my lawyer and Annie would be informed, and that would mean more time away from my girls. I sigh and stare at the cop, noticing the ring on his finger. On the other hand, I can set her sights on another man and get rid of her once and for all.

I know what the clever thing to do would be...

"It's not what you think," I try one last time.

"It never is, now, final warning."

I turn back to Amy. "This isn't over," I warn her. But she just smiles at me and turns towards the officer.

"Miss, are you okay?" he repeats as I dissolve into the darkness, and she walks out of the shadows.

Have you enjoyed reading this story? You don't want to miss Four Rooms!

If you enjoyed The Sweetest Thing, please consider leaving a review on Amazon and Goodreads.

Stay up to date on new releases and exclusive content. Sign up now for my Newsletter!

A WORD FROM JANE

I would like to start by thanking you the reader, so much for reading! If you enjoyed the story, please leave a review and recommend the book to any friend you think would love this story. You will have my eternal love and gratitude.

A massive thank you to Tracey Caldwell, your input and encouragement has been amazing as always you inspire me in more ways than one, can't wait for those beach Mai Tais and long black boots ;)

Margot – thanks for the sprints the laughs and the encouragement – love you Ladyface.

To K – As always without your direction, comments and segues my writing will be no where near what it is or could be. You drive me to do better and get through the mountain... one day it will actually all happen... Thanks tyrant.

ABOUT THE AUTHOR

Jane Wynters doesn't quite know how to answer the question of "where are you from?" She's moved from place to place like a snowflake on the wind always searching for a safe place to land. She loves meeting new people and exploring new places. She loves reading, writing and conjuring new worlds from her imagination. Coffee is at the top of her food pyramid and she is fluent in three languages, her favourite being sarcasm.

Want to know more about the author and keep in touch? Get snippets of upcoming books and have a bit of twisted fun?

Come join me inWonderland...
Sign up for my newsletter

ALSO BY J. A. WYNTERS

Standalone

Guarding Gabriel

The Sweetest Thing

The Beverage Wars

Mai Tais and Goodbyes

Fractured

Losing Liam

Four Rooms

The Sweetest Thing

The Parts of Me Series

Spare Parts, Book 1

Fixed Parts, Book 2

Broken Parts, Book 3

Coming Soon...

Torn Apart, Book 4

Picked Apart, Book 5

The Fractured Fairytale Series

Beast

Wolf

Hunter

Dreamer